A Nov

Fault Line©

T. L. Scott

Copyright February 25, 2018

i

Fault Line©

A Novel by T. L. Scott

This story is dedicated to all those brave men and women who put themselves in harm's way to keep us safe.

Those who made the choice to join the military, police, or federal law enforcement. We are all safer because of your diligence and sacrifices while on the watch- Thank You.

Fault Line©

A Novel by T. L. Scott

Chapter 1

Late summer is a wonderful time of year. The sun has
eased back from the blistering intensity of July. It now warms the
skin instead of frying it like an egg in a skillet. The air has lost
some of its sweltering quality. A cool breeze stirs the air and then
rolls gently through the park.

This green oasis of nature is a favorite place for kids of all
ages. People play catch with Frisbees, while others toss a
baseball back and forth. Tired mothers stand at the ready,
keeping a watchful eye on their tireless toddlers at play. Young
couples lay on blankets, basking in the sun as much as they are
basking in their love. People feed the ducks by the pond. Joggers
make their way along the path which winds around the
promenade and continues on its serpentine route through the
park. The rhythmic cadence of their footfalls add to the natural
rhythm of the day. At the south-eastern corner, a black lab races

along the green expanse of grass and launches into the air to catch a Frisbee with effortless grace.

Bill is taking it all in. It feels good to be back home. The smell of fresh-cut grass combined with the morning breeze helps him to relax like he hasn't been able to do for so long.

"Man, you gotta get the Shelby. If you're going to get a Mustang, you might as well get the best," said Sam. He was from Virginia Beach and had grown up around muscle cars. His dad taught him some of life's most valuable lessons while tinkering under the hood of one project after another. When it came to cars, Sam knew what he was talking about. His favorite project had been rebuilding a 442 with his dad and uncle. It was the first time his dad had involved him in the restoration of the engine and transmission. Before that, he'd mostly done body work and been the one to fetch what the men needed. In fact, looking back, it was that restoration more than anything else which had led him to decide on being a 63B, light vehicle mechanic.

"Listen, man," said Sebastian, "I still haven't made up my mind. Yeah, I love the Shelby, but that Camaro is awesome too." He held up his hands to forestall the complaints he knew were coming. "Before you say that it can't compare with the Mustang, think about after-market work. With some fine tuning and a little tweak to the computer chip, she'd be sweet! Now toss in a new transmission, and it would scream!" Sebastian was an Army brat and had spent most of his childhood in Germany. He had always been good with electronics and had initially come into the Army to do that. Once he was in the Army, he learned about the things the guys in EOD did so he cross-trained and became an 89D.

"It still wouldn't be the same," grumbled Sam.

"To tell you the truth, I'm leaning toward the Beamer. I've been reading about the M3, and it's a complete package. I like the way it rides so low to the ground. It really hugs the road." Sebastian scooted to the edge of his chair while he was talking. "It's got 425 horsepower pushing around 4,000 pounds. Get this man, it goes zero to sixty in four-point-five seconds!"

"Your right man," said Tommy, "that M3 is sweet." He was leaning back as usual. His pose and attitude, as usual, was relaxed. "For me though, I'm going to get a Range Rover."

Tommy was from Atlanta and would be going there to visit his mother after the wedding. Like the rest of the guys, he hadn't been home in over eight months. He was an only child and in-spite-of his tough exterior, he had a soft spot for his mother. She had made a lot of sacrifices for him. His dad died when he was young, and she'd raised him as a single mother. He owed her a lot and tried to respect her sacrifices by becoming the best man he could be. He had big shoes to fill. His father had been a great man. Tommy constantly strove to become better. One day maybe someone would think that he'd been a great man as well.

"You're all crazy," said Raul. "The classics are the best. I'm gonna get me a '78 Monte Carlo and trick it out. Picture it man, lime green, chrome rims, at least 32's, and full hydraulics, a true hopper." He crossed his arms and sat back with a smug look on his face. When none of the guys showed any reaction, he quickly sat forward on his chair again and put his hands on his knees.

"You've got to be shittin' me guys. You don't know what a hopper is?" He held his hand out, palm down, and bounced it up and down, small at first then bigger and bigger. "Sweet right?" he asked, leaning back again with a big smile.

A Novel by T. L. Scott

Raul was a proud New Yorker. As much as he loved his city, he knew he had to leave her to find himself. He'd seen too many friends die over stupid things. He wasn't afraid to die. Dying was easy, he wanted to make something of himself. That was hard. He had to work at it all the time.

He knew what he needed to do the first time he heard a presentation by an Army recruiter. He'd never been good at school. He wasn't bad at it; he was a C student. He just wasn't interested in what they were teaching him.

Most of his teachers tried about as hard as the kids. Everybody was coasting through. School was a place he had to go to so he could get out of there. He knew that drop-outs never got away. He had to finish High School so he could get away and make a difference. The Army needed soldiers. It turned out to be a good match.

Once he enlisted, he decided he liked the camaraderie and worked hard to become better. He graduated at or near the top of his classes. He found that he liked to learn. It was different than school back at home. This was stuff he wanted to know. The instructors really cared about teaching you. They got up close and personal. The lessons were going to keep him and his buddies alive. He decided to try some college classes after he settled into his first posting at Fort Bragg. He finished his Bachelor's degree in three years and was working on his Masters in Adverse Psychology. Along the way, he also completed Army Sniper training. He had a real knack for observing and analyzing. He was also very good at taking action when it was the right time.

Bill sat back and listened. He was usually the quiet one of the group. These were his friends, and he knew he was damn lucky to have them. It was funny that two years ago they hadn't known each other. They came from different walks of life. Each man had decided to join for his own reasons. At the core of it, they were looking for the same thing. Each of them wanted to become better than what they were. They'd become as close as any brothers. Being in battle together does that; especially when they'd saved each other's lives too many times to count.

Bill watched the tranquil scene of normal life play out in the park across the street. A large, black crow was working on a crust of bread. It would attack the prize a few times with its beak, then raise its head, darting it from side to side to make sure his perimeter was clear. The crow was cautious. He made sure his prize was still safely his. Satisfied, it returned its attention to the bread, stabbing its beak into the crusty morsel. Suddenly, it dropped the meal and launched into the air.

The unmistakable crack of a gunshot shattered the tranquility.

Instinct and experience guided Bill's eyes over his left shoulder. Reflex and muscle training guided him as he gracefully turned his body, rising fluidly off the chair, his eyes searching for the aggressor. He dropped to a kneeling position to minimize his exposure to the potential aggressor. His right knee hadn't made contact with the red bricks of the patio before his eyes locked on the target. His right hand clasped the grip of his Sig Sauer SP 2022 Nitron. Having identified his target, he began clearing it from the holster. His left arm, now clear of the seatback, came around for a two-handed grip. His sights locked on the confirmed threat.

A man stood over a woman in the middle of the two-lane road. She was down on her knees, gesturing with her hands

Fault Line©

fiercely. Bill couldn't make out the words they were saying from this distance, but it was obvious he wasn't asking her out on a date. The man was holding the stock of what looked like an AK 47 with his right hand, waving it around menacingly, while shouting at the woman. His long, stringy, brown hair whipped around his head. He punctuated his agitation by thrusting the gun up and down.

The woman raised up off her heels and said something. Whatever she said caught his attention. He closed the distance between them then bent his thin frame down so his face was inches from hers.

She shrank back from his leering face. Whatever it was she said next, he must have found amusing. He tossed his head back and laughed, then started dancing around her. He was doing a kind of high-step, his knees pumping high while he jabbed the rifle sharply up and down. He was really getting it too. He completed his circle of her and stomped his heavy boot down, ending his dance. He threw his head back and howled like a wolf. Bill had to give it to him; the guy had some good lungs.

A Novel by T. L. Scott

The man took in a deep breath as he rolled his body back forward. He snugged the butt of the gun into his shoulder and sighted in on the woman. The black barrel ended inches from her upturned face. Her jet-black hair blew back from her face in the gentle breeze. It, and the angle she was facing prevented Bill from seeing her face.

Bill admired the way she faced the man that was about to take her life. She looked proud and strong. Even if she was seconds from meeting her maker, she wasn't going to cower. He respected her for that.

Bill increased the pressure of his trigger finger. Seeing the man tense his shoulder and bring his right elbow out to the side triggered Bill to engage fully. A split second before applying the final amount of pressure, the dancer jerked to the right. He fell in what seemed like slow motion, Bill knew better it was what he called battle speed. Bullets sprayed out from the barrel of the AK47 in a deadly arc. It was good that the rifle shot up to six hundred rounds-per-minute. It quickly ran out of ammo before anyone was hurt by this madman. With the guy out of the fight, Bill scanned for more threats. Seeing none, he did a quick check on his friends. Sam and Raul were both covering down on the baddie.

Bill kept his weapon trained on the inert form in the road, from his kneeling position. He cut his eyes over to Tommy and Sebastian and saw they were taking cover behind the decorative fence that separated the café from the sidewalk. He could see they were at a loss. They were used to being in uniform and reacting as they were trained to do. When their finely-honed reactions came up with a missing weapon, they didn't have an answer for a beat. This wasn't Iraq or Afghanistan; it was Texas, and yet war had found them here.

Bill kept his weapon pointed at the bad guy as he ran over to the woman. She was still on her knees in the middle of the road. The man hadn't moved since he'd hit the pavement. Bill saw why. A pool of blood spread out from his head. The blood looked black on the asphalt road. A smaller puddle was congealing under his torso as well. Bill wasn't taking any chances. He'd seen men get up from wounds that should've killed them outright before.

A Novel by T. L. Scott

He slowly circled the body, keeping his eyes on the man's hands. If they so much as twitched, Bill would drop the hammer. His finger skillfully had four of the seven pounds of pressure squeezing the match grade trigger. It would only take a small fraction more to dispatch the man if needed. He kicked the rifle away from the corpse and then looked at the woman. She was staring at the body.

Bill couldn't see her face from his angle. Her black hair was loose and partially covered it. He could see that she was shivering in-spite-of the warm air.

A crowd was beginning to form. Sam and Raul were still training their weapons around, searching for any more potential threats. Sebastian and Tommy were keeping the small crowd that had formed back, maintaining a loose perimeter defense. They were doing their best to keep the look-e-loos away from the scene. Of course, in this modern day, most of the people had their phones out, trying to catch it all on video. It would be up on social media before the authorities had a chance to arrive on the scene.

"Are you okay ma'am?"

She raised her obsidian eyes to his and said in a calm voice, "I think so."

"Are you hurt?" Bill asked her.

"No, . . . I don't think so," she replied shaking her head slowly.

"Are there any more of them?" He asked as he cast his eyes around.

"I don't know," answered the woman. "I don't know who he is."

She looked down at her lap, and her body sagged down. The steel that had held her up seemed to leave her. "He was really going to kill me," she murmured.

They both knew she'd spoken the truth. Bill didn't see any need to say anything further on that point.

"What's your name ma'am?" He asked her in a gentle tone as he reached out his hand to help her up.

She took it and let him help her to her feet. Once she was sure she wasn't going to fall back down, she squeezed his hand a little and responded; "My name is Isabella, thank you." She said looking him in the eye.

"You're welcome," he replied simply.

There was something about this woman, something more than her beauty. There was a feeling of strength that radiated from her. He tore his gaze from her beautiful eyes and looked around at the scene developing around them.

More people had gathered on the sidewalks on both sides of the street. Traffic was at a standstill. Cars were lined up with their doors standing open. Their drivers had abandoned them to get a better look at the aftermath of the violence that had played out in their small town. Small children were standing with their parents. Some parents were trying to cover their children's eyes, but the curious little ones weren't having it. Bill wished he could cover the body up. Not to give the man his dignity but to lessen the macabre interest that had overtaken these people. He knew better though; he knew the police were going to conduct an investigation. Back here, that meant collecting forensic evidence. As if on cue, the shrill notes of a siren cut through the still morning air. All together, less than three minutes had passed since the first shot had been fired, and the discordant wail sounded the arrival of law and order.

Fault Line©

Chapter 2

In the time it took for that terrible scene to play out, on what ironically was Main Street, the crow had made it to the edge of the small town, and a very bad man knew that things had changed.

Sound travels well over the dry air. To a trained ear there is no mistaking the crack of a rifle. When a person was as experienced with weapons as this particular man was, they can even tell the type of rifle fired.

He knew the sound had likely come from one of his men. The wind whispered the story into his well-trained ear. The answering report of pistols told the next chapter. It was the ensuing silence which told him the conclusion of this drama had played out. His man was probably dead. If not dead, then he would soon be locked up in a jail cell. Regardless, the heat had just been cranked up several degrees.

The warehouse he was standing in was far enough from the road that it avoided attention and was still close enough for quick transportation of the goods he traded in. It had proved to be a good place for a temporary headquarters. It had hills on three sides with the front opening out to the road in the distance. The road leading into it wound down into this valley. The warehouse had been built up, so it sat higher than the ground around it to prevent the products stored inside getting damaged during the few times it rained heavily.

He looked out at the gravel road which cut its way out to highway 27. His eye caught the movement of a single bird. It flew, rising on the air that was heating as the sun cut higher into the sky. He stood in the entrance to the warehouse for a few minutes, just letting his eyes and thoughts wander. In time, he saw a cloud of dust rising from the gravel road.

"Have him brought up to the office," he said to his men that were stationed on each side of the door, their weapons at the ready.

He made his way to the east side of the building and looked over his operation as he went. A group of his men was loosely gathered by the trucks. Some of them were working on the engines, but most were just standing around and talking.

Fault Line©

Another group was gathered around the cages on the other side of the building. He heard some tell-tale sounds coming from the smaller administrative offices. He didn't care if the men had some fun, as long as they didn't damage the product.

Everything seemed to be under control. He climbed the metal stairs to the office, noting the positions of the guards that were up on the rafters. One of the men noticed him and gave a small wave. Miguel forced a smile on his hard face and returned the salute. He had learned over time that some men responded better if there was a sense of camaraderie. All Miguel cared about was that the men did what he told them to and were loyal. Whatever it took to make that happen, he would do.

Once inside the air-conditioned space, he fired up his laptop and started making calls on his phone. He needed answers and knew that the fastest way to get them was to check out social media. He had become friends on several of the local pages. As he had believed, the American love for posting what they saw, heard, thought, or believed online told him what he wanted to know.

A Novel by T. L. Scott

This wasn't a big hit to the operation. It could be handled, with some small interventions at the right levels. An unstable man, high on meth, goes berserk on Main Street. That would be a good cover. It was sensational and yet believable. It was also not far from the truth. There would be a price to pay for this. He had to send a message to the rest of his men that this was not going to be tolerated. They had to stay focused on their jobs and, above all else, stay invisible.

His guest was coming to get an update on the operation. The man had been useful while setting up this operation but he had to be put in his place. He thought that his public standing afforded him a right to control how things were handled. He had to be made to understand that he wasn't in charge. He was only a tool to be used. He was still a useful tool, so he had to take care of him and handle him appropriately. A time was coming when his position and sources would no longer be necessary. He would then be discarded. Today was not that day, but it wasn't far away.

"How in the hell did this happen," the man demanded to know. "You said there wouldn't be any problems. You said there wouldn't be anything to worry about," he said, pacing back and forth. He was really worked up. His face was turning red.

Miguel enjoyed watching the man work himself up. When he talked the skin under his chin flopped around. It made Miguel think about the waddle on a turkey. He fought to control his smile.

"Well, guess what? I'm fucking worried." The man stopped and braced his hands on the table opposite Miguel. "I thought you had control over that group of fuck-ups!" he demanded. The man's voice had a plaintive note to it that wasn't present when he was talking to the press.

Miguel knew this man liked to be in control. He wasn't in control of this and was just beginning to realize how little control he had.

"Careful amigo, you wouldn't want someone to hear you? They might question your loyalties. You wouldn't want that would you?" he asked as he leveled his gaze on the agitated man.

The man glared at Miguel. He didn't like to be challenged. That hard look melted away under the cold stare that was locked on him. He could feel the cold blue eyes as they bored into his soul. They held no compassion, no warmth. They were dead eyes and until that gaze passed the man couldn't breathe.

"Come, sit down, have a drink. All this pacing and shouting will not change what has happened. It changes nothing." Miguel waved his hand dismissively. He picked up the bottle from the silver serving tray. It was such a contrast, the fine silver sitting on the beat-up scarred wood of the table. The man poured the liquor into the fine cut crystal tumbler, carefully measuring out precisely three fingers worth. Once the liquor was poured, he raised his eyes to the man who was still standing.

"I said sit down."

He didn't raise his voice. He didn't need to. His voice, like his eyes, held no compassion.

"You know," Miguel said once his guest was seated, "I have come to truly appreciate fine Scotch. Many of my countrymen only drink tequila."

He slid the tumbler across the table. "Now, don't get me wrong my friend, I like my tequila too, but a fine scotch, now, that is something else altogether. You see, tequila is like a scorpion. It comes right out and stares you in the eye. It says fuck you *esse* and then it stings your ass. It might kill you. It will make you sick. But you definitely will remember its bite. Now, take this fine Scotch, it has a bite as well," he said pointing at the tumbler. Condensation was forming on the side of the glass.

"The difference is that it starts out with a smooth burn that slowly engulfs all of you. It does not sting you," he said, shaking his head.

He quickly leaned forward, placing his hands on the side of the glass, the ropy muscles in his forearms flexing as he pressed his hands down on the table. "It consumes you. It consumes you, and you don't even realize it until it is too late."

"You see my friend that is what we have done here. We moved slowly. We took our time, set things up one step at a time. We are here. This is our town," he said, sweeping his arm in the general direction of the town. "This problem on Main Street is only a small bump in the road," he said as he dismissively waved his hand. "Yes, we will be careful, but we do not need to stop our operation."

A Novel by T. L. Scott

"Drink up my friend and let the beast warm your heart," Miguel told him as he leaned back in his chair.

The Senator drank down the Scotch, but the chill from his friend's eyes tamped out the fire of the beast. In fact, he'd never felt so cold in his life. He knew that the man had spoken the truth. The beast had consumed him, and there was no going back again.

Fault Line©

Chapter 3

"Alright, Bill," Sheriff Olsen said as he walked into the interrogation room.

Bill noted that he didn't close the door behind him.

"I think we've kept you boys here long enough. The witnesses corroborated your story. Enough of them told their version of the story the same way, or near enough as to make no difference that you and your boys said it happened. You likely saved some lives here today." He paused before continuing and propped his bony rump on the edge of the table, across from Bill. "As much as I appreciate your help, I want you to know that I don't like having shots fired on Main Street."

When the sheriff didn't hear a response, he continued. "You boys are back here for Julie and Tom's wedding, I reckon'. How long do you plan on sticking around after it's over?"

"I'll be staying on for about a week. My friends will be going to see their families on Sunday. We all just want to take a break and enjoy our leave for a while."

"I don't see as there should be a problem with that." Sheriff Olsen said as he hitched his thumbs in his gun belt. "I just like to know who in my town is carrying and knows how to use them."

"Sheriff, most of the people in this town, men and women, fit that description."

"That's true, Bill." Sheriff Olsen agreed as he slowly nodded as if he was going over a list in his head of all the people in the area that had weapons at their disposal. "You know as well as I do, though, that there are people who know how to shoot and then there are those that are good at it." He went on. "You and your friends definitely fall in the second group."

"Sheriff, you've known me my whole life. I'm here to see my little sister get married. I'm glad we were in the right place today to make sure that whoever that guy was didn't hurt anyone. We're not looking for trouble. All we want to do is relax and have some fun before we have to go back. How's the woman doing anyway?"

"She's okay, all things considered. We're still trying to piece together why that guy was in town and waving around a fully automatic AK47. We don't know why he picked her to fight with. There's a lot about this that we don't have the answers to yet," he said as he cast his eyes over to the wall. A couple seconds passed before he continued in a firm tone, "we'll get to the bottom of it."

"She claims that she never saw the man before today; said she's just passing through town and stopped for a little break. She was drinking coffee at the same café you and your friends were sitting at. She says that she saw him looking at her while she had a coffee but didn't think anything of it."

Bill didn't fail to notice how closely the sheriff was watching him for any reaction. His weathered face was deeply tanned. The cheekbones stood out in stark contrast to the hollows beneath them. His dark brown eyes were edged with deep wrinkles.

"A woman that looks like her has to deal with guys always looking at her, so that makes sense. Anyway, when she left the café, she said that she knew the guy was following her. Who knows, maybe in his mind they shared some kind of *moment* while he was staring at her. She said that she thought he would get the message if she kept on walking. She didn't think she was in any trouble. It was broad daylight, and she was in front of all those people. Right before she got to the car, he grabbed her by the shoulder and spun her around. She said that he demanded to know where she thought she was going. She tried to get away from him, but he wasn't having it. She said his eyes looked huge and he kept glancing everywhere at once."

"He was probably on something, we figure. We'll know for sure once the toxicology report comes back. Of course, we know the cause of death, but in these cases, there has to be an autopsy anyway."

The sheriff paused, and Bill could actually see the wall come up. The set of his face changed over to bureaucratic neutral cold so fast it was disconcerting. Bill knew that was the end of the chat.

"Make sure your friends don't get in any more trouble, Bill. If we have more questions for you or your friends, I guess we know where we can find you."

"Yes Sir, we're staying out at the farm."

Fault Line©

"That's fine, son. I am sorry that this happened. You boys have seen enough war. I want you to know that I appreciate what you're doing over there. Tell your dad I said hello." With that, Sheriff Olsen got up and walked out of the room.

Bill followed him out. Something about the conversation wasn't right. He just couldn't put his finger on it. The sheriff had been sincere about the last part. Everything before that though, Bill felt that he had been holding something back. He was going over the conversation in his mind trying to find what had given him that odd feeling. The feeling that Sheriff Olsen wasn't telling him everything was strong. Then again, he reasoned, he is the sheriff and would know things that could connect to any number of things he told himself. Still though, something had felt . . . well, *wrong* somehow. It felt for some reason like he had an idea why that guy had been in town and wasn't too surprised that he had gotten himself dead.

Bill had fallen back from the sheriff. About five feet separated them. He had no illusions that Sheriff Olsen had forgotten about him. He had dismissed him and was moving on with his day. That didn't mean that he would allow Bill to wander around the station unchecked.

Bill followed the sheriff out to the front of the station. He walked down the corridor and passed several open doors along the way. Three of the rooms he passed looked exactly like the one he had just left. They had the same cheap rectangular dark gray metal table flanked by one chair on the far side and two chairs on the side closest to the door. His own experience had shown him that the chairs were bolted to the floor. It made sense, he reflected. One of those chairs had probably been used as a weapon at some point in time. That was the reason for most modifications in his experience. We learn from our mistakes, all too often the kind of mistake that led to someone bleeding. Hopefully not fatally. Maybe that was the reason the table top was stainless steel? It would be easier to clean up than some other materials.

The walls along the corridor were painted a tired white with a trim of what once was a yellow line. The tile on the floor clearly showed wear down the middle. You could even see where the path led into the other rooms. It was evident which interrogation room was used the most. It was the first one from the front of the station. Bill could tell because the tiles were almost worn out going into that room. We are all creatures of habit and all too often follow the path of least resistance. In this case, the closest room to get the business over with.

One of the doors was shut. He assumed it was probably the room for monitoring the interrogations. He was right. It was a communications suite that monitored the video and audio feeds from each of the three interrogation rooms plus all the cameras throughout the station to include the ones in the basement overlooking the six holding cells. It also held the router for the internal computers in the station, the backup drives from the internal and external security system, and the on-site recordings of the 911 system. In essence, this was truly the bullpen. Even if the silly humans insisted on saying the space eleven feet away, which was manned by Officer Stacy Ortega, was the bullpen.

Bill had always been good at noticing the small things. His time outside the wire had honed that skill to a fine edge. Not much escaped his sharp eyes.

When Bill arrived at the receiving area of the station, he saw his friends. They were standing around and waiting. That was one thing that being in the military taught you to do well, how to wait. The same sergeant was behind the desk talking on the phone, just as she had been when they arrived. The same two cops were at their desks, behind her, working on their computers.

Bill reflected on how strange it was that things stayed the same even though so much else had changed. It wasn't solely due to the amount of time that had passed since they had entered the door of the Police Station. Bill knew that life outside of these walls had moved on, but yet, here, inside, it almost seemed as if they existed in their own unique microcosm of space and time. One could almost believe that when they left these walls things would be exactly as it was when they entered. Bill knew this illusion for the transparent image it was. The difference was that him and his friends were moving out of the station now, where before they were graciously *escorted* inside.

The only other remarkable difference was that Lieutenant Gonzalez was chatting with Sam. Gonzalez's body language showed that he was at ease and he had an easy smile on his face. For all, it looked like he was just sharing war stories with some fellow soldiers. Although they were soldiers of a different uniform, they were not all that different in the end. When you stared down the business end of a weapon from the wrong side it kind of bound you together. There was a sense of kinsmanship amongst those that had been in harm's way. That was definitely true between cops and the military. In fact, most cops had been in the military at one point.

Bill knew Jorge Gonzalez since they were in the fourth grade. That was when Jorge's family moved to Greenville from Arizona. They knew each other but had never actually become friends.

Jorge had played on the same teams as Bill, and there had always been a kind of rivalry between them. The truth was, they were quite a bit alike. In fact, they were too much alike to be friends. They were both good at sports and invariably were selected to be the captains of the opposing teams. When they were on the same teams, they were competing against each other to see who could do better. Bill had been the wide receiver on the football team. Jorge had been the tail-back. They were both good and fast, but Jorge was more muscular where Bill had the height advantage. Their rivalry was one that was built on respect. They were both good guys, and they respected the skills of the other. That didn't mean that they liked each other.

The animosity all went back to their junior year. Of course, it was over a girl. It had to be over a girl. What else could spur such strong feelings so many years later? Of course, it didn't help when the girl ended up with Jorge in the end. Not in the junior year, mind you. Bill had won that time. But, in the end, she was sleeping in Jorge's bed while Bill, more often than not, was curled up with his gun someplace most people had never and would never, hear about.

One thing about Jorge that Bill had always respected though was his integrity. He was never one to take an easy short-cut. He liked to do things the right way. Bill supposed that it was one of the reasons that he had become a cop. Well, that and the fact his dad and uncle had been cops. Jorge's dad had died in the line of duty in Arizona. Jorge didn't talk about it, but somehow everyone knew anyway. That was the way things worked in small towns. Somehow everyone just knew everyone else's business, or so they thought.

The sheriff stood on the top step of the station watching Bill and his friends climb into his truck. The light breeze ruffled his mostly gray hair. Traffic had returned to normal around the promenade. People were going about their business as if nothing had happened. It was the picture of small-town life. The little smile on his face gave an impression of ease to the citizens who looked up to him. He cast a friendly wave back.

"So, what do you think Jorge," asked Sheriff Olsen as he heard his deputy walk up behind him.

"Well, I believe it went down just like they said. I don't think they were up to anything. Still, I don't like having more guns in town."

"I know what you mean," agreed Sheriff Olsen. "I don't want anybody taking the law into their own hands. I know them boys can handle themselves. I also believe that they will do the right thing if faced with a situation. They proved that today. The part that bothers me is that we are the ones that have to answer why we were not the ones to drop that guy."

"We can take care of this one Sheriff. I don't think anyone will look too closely at it. The stories are all pretty much the same from all the witnesses. Bill's friends saved that woman's life. They did the right thing. This is Texas, not California anyway. The fact we had some boys with weapons is normal here."

"I know you're right," said the sheriff, "but I still don't feel good about it. Let's keep a close eye on things till they move on out of town Jorge. I have a bad feeling that this is not the end. I feel more trouble on the way. I hope I'm wrong and it is only my old bones complaining."

The men stood on the front steps of the police station. Each one looking down the street. The scene was a typical small town. People were going about their business. White fluffy clouds slowly moved across the deep blue sky. Despite this normal setting, they could both feel something ominous brewing, something more than the storm they were talking about on the news.

Fault Line©

The sheriff broke the silence. "I'm going to go for a cruise. Hold down things here till I get back," he said as he walked away to get into his cruiser.

Jorge went back inside the station. He was the shift commander, and it was his responsibility to run things. He glanced up at the clock on the wall. *Wow*, he thought to himself, *not even two yet*. The clock was hung over the entrance to the corridor leading to the interrogation rooms and then on to the holding cells. There weren't many cells for a town this size. Three cells on each side. They were more than they had needed since Jorge joined the force eleven years ago. In all that time there was only once that all the cells had people in them. It was when the big bar-fight out at *The Thorny Cactus* went down. Even then, it was nothing more serious than some drunks acting up after a wanna-be biker gang passing through town picked the wrong place to pick a fight. In reality, it was pretty funny, looking back at it. The bikers had been well into their 50's and beyond and looked more like suits than hardened gang members. As it turned out, they were mostly lawyers from Phoenix who were out for a joyride and decided to take on more than they could handle.

The sheriff let the whole bunch out at sunrise, once they'd sobered up. No charges were pressed since they had all pooled their money to pay for the damages to *The Thorny Cactus*.

The town was usually quiet. Jorge and the rest of the force did their best to keep it that way. It was a good town to live in, and they tried to keep it that way too.

Fault Line©

Chapter 4

The mood around the fire was somber. They'd finished dinner and were taking it easy watching the sun as it dipped below the horizon. It was just the guys for now. Bill's parents were in the house tidying up the kitchen. Bill knew that they were taking their time to give the guys time to themselves.

"I'm gonna go to this place called the Watershed. You can't believe how good the fried chicken is there. It tastes so good. Man, I'm literally drooling just thinking about it." Tommy leaned further back in the high-backed wooden chair with a very contented look on his face.

"Man, that sounds good brother," Sam exclaimed. "You got me thinking about this little place, and I do mean little, there ain't more than six tables in the place. They've got this seafood platter." He paused, lost in the memory for a minute. "They bring it out on a real platter, no shit, it's this big around," he said making a circle out of his arms at least as big as a car tire. He inhaled deeply through his nose as if he could smell the delicacies all over again. "They have the catch of the day in the middle of the platter. Bro', I'm telling you they have the whole fish, right there. Around that they have fried clams, shrimp steamed and fried, steamed mussels, raw oysters, and get this- the best crab cakes this side of heaven."

"Sebastian, how about you brother," asked Tommy after taking a long pull from his beer.

"You know me, brother. I'm a carnivore through and through. Just give me a good steak and some potatoes, and I'm good-to-go," he said, reaching over and clinking bottles with Tommy.

Bill was listening to his friends with half an ear. He kept running over the conversation he'd had with the sheriff earlier. It still didn't sit well with him, and he couldn't quite figure out why. All he could come up with was that the sheriff was holding something back. Of course, he was. Why was that bothering him?

He couldn't help thinking about the sheriff's son Daniel. They'd been good friends growing up. Daniel spent a good bit of time out on the ranch. His mom had died when he was little, and his dad's hours were long. Even small-town sheriffs had to work all hours of the day and night.

When Bill was in the fifth grade his dad brought on a new hand. Michael had owned his own dairy farm until something happened, and he lost it. Bill's dad had helped him out and gave him the job. It came with an apartment over the barn where he stayed with his son, Dave.

Dave was a few years older than Bill. The boys became close. The three of them learned how to hunt and fish together. They learned how to drive the tractor and how to plow a field under the watchful eye of Bill's dad. As they grew up, Bill and Daniel started to realize that their friend was a little different. Even though he was older, they were in the same class up to the seventh grade. Other kids called Dave slow. Some called him a retard. Well, behind his back they did. Nobody dared call him that to his face. Even for his age, Dave was big. The kids in their class were three years younger and nowhere near his size.

When the school decided to hold him back, yet again, from going into the eighth grade, Michael made the decision to keep him at home. For a few years, Dave studied with a tutor and was homeschooled. He did better studying that way. The tutor was good, and Dave made progress. In time, he got tired of studying books and told his dad that he wanted to just work on the farm.

Dan was the first one to talk about joining the Army and going to war. The fight against terrorism was in full swing, and he was ready to defend his country. They practiced their shooting and hunting skills and watched all the movies they could to prepare them.

By the time they were juniors, the decision was pretty much made. They had already talked to their parents about enlisting. It wasn't a hard sell. Bill and Dave's dads had been in the Army, and Dan's had been a Marine. When it came to serving their country, they had a long and proud family history.

The boys studied the ASVAB study guide for months. It wasn't for Dan or Bill. Both of them had good grades in school. Of course, the preparation for the test could only help. No, they were trying to help Dave get his score high enough to pass.

After months of hard work, Dave eventually scored high enough on the screening test to take the real one at the Military

Fault Line©

Entrance Processing Center. The boys were excited. They had waited for this day to come. They were all going to join together.

Dave was mad at the world when the Army told him that he wasn't qualified to enlist. He hadn't scored high enough on the test. He couldn't understand why they didn't want him. He told Bill over some cold beers. "I'm a good shot, I'm strong, and I'm good at following orders. It ain't fair Bill. I'd be a good soldier."

"I know you would be. I don't know what they were thinking. The recruiter said you could try again in a couple of months."

"Aw Bill, you know that won't make any difference. I worked really hard to learn that stuff," he said. He was a big man that looked like a little boy. He sat there, on the porch, with his head hanging low and his hands just dangling between his knees. The big man looked beat.

"Hey, look at it this way though, it's their loss and this way you don't need to leave Anna."

A smile spread across Dave's face. He really did love her. She loved him too. They had been together for five years and when Dave told her that he was going to join the Army she had refused to talk to him for a week. Bill had never seen his friend so upset. The big guy's heart was breaking. Finally, Anna broke down and they had a long talk. Dave told Bill that night that he proposed to her. In time Anna said yes.

Bill and Dan, as expected, had passed their tests and enlisted in the delayed entry under the buddy program. When the day came for the boys to go to basic training, Dave wrapped them both in his big arms and gave them a hug. He wished with all his heart that he could be going with them. Seeing Anna standing off to the side made it possible for him to get through it.

Bill and Dan were guaranteed to stay together as long as they both passed their courses. They had no trouble doing that. They were at the top of their classes academically and physically.

The time came for their first deployment to the war zone. They'd been trained for what to expect. No matter how good the training is, you know it's just training. Actually, being out on patrol for the first time made it real. It was a good thing they were with seasoned veterans. Seeing how calm they were helped them contain their nearly frantic nerves. They didn't come under fire on that first outing. In fact, it didn't happen until their fifth patrol outside the wire. By then, they were used to the routine. The threat was quickly eliminated by the lead element, and neither of the boys returned fire on the enemy.

They'd been in theater for just over seven months and were out on another routine early morning patrol. Bill knew that statistically, it was the safest time of day. All night long Jihad Johny had lobbed mortars at them. They usually didn't land inside the wall. It was crazy, but after a while, you got used to the shells detonating so close to you that everything shook, and yet, you barely woke up unless the warning sounded.

As usual, there weren't many people up and about at this time of day. The first call to prayer had already sounded, and people were going about their morning routines. That was what made this war so hard to understand. Most of the people were just regular people that just wanted to go about their lives. The fanatics knew it and hid among them, using them for cover. It made it nearly impossible to know who was a threat and who wasn't. There was only one way to stay alive: everybody was a threat. They were a suspected threat until they revealed themselves to be a known threat. Shooting at you was a sure sign that someone was a known threat. Driving a car at you at high-speed turned the driver to a threat. Threats were everywhere, in every doorway, in every window, in every alleyway. There was only one way to make it through: trust your team and trust your training.

They were approaching the last quadrant of their patrol grid when they started taking fire from a rooftop. Bill knew that they had oversight protection from somewhere. He had no idea where and no way to know if they had a shot. He pushed his back against the wall to minimize his target area. He was pushing so hard that he thought he was going to push through into the house. He wasn't joking. He'd seen how some of these places were built.

The squad fell back and took up a defensive position. The shooter was still trying to get to them. His bullets gouged out chunks of the wall about a half a meter over their heads. Bill felt like they were relatively safe where they were.

Fault Line©

That feeling evaporated when a dark-colored car blocked off the end of the road and opened fire on his team. Bill hit the deck and returned fire. They were pinned down. If they fled, the shooter on the roof would pick them off. If they stayed where they were, they'd be cut to ribbons.

Bill took out two of the shooters right away. Two more were still taking random shots at them. They must have hardened the car doors. The bullets weren't punching through to the occupants inside. The terrorists had learned a trick or two along the way. They were raising their rifles and spraying the lethal bursts in the soldier's general direction. The walls funneled the bullets toward them.

Bill started hearing a lesson from his training: Move or Die. He didn't want to die, and there wasn't any place to move to! He popped to his feet and pushed his back against the opposite wall he'd been against moments before. The shooter on the roof still couldn't get an angle on his location. Likewise, Bill couldn't get a bead on him either.

One shooter stayed in the car. He was shooting more sparingly, taking his time. Why? Why's he taking his time? Why is the one on the roof still shooting even though he knows he can't hit us?

"Move! Move! Move!" he yelled to the rest of his team. He ran across the road and hit the double wooden doors with a front kick. The doors burst open. The force of Bill's kick knocked the door on the right to the ground. The hinges ripped free from the wall. The other door fell as well, but one of the hinges stubbornly remained embedded in the wall. The wood panel door lay at an angle across the entrance to the courtyard.   Bill kept going, following through with his momentum, into the small yard.

It was no more than a patch of dirt with a half-dozen or so chickens flying crazily around. He tracked for hostiles. Seeing none, he didn't engage. He saw a door on the left and angled over to it, not letting up on his speed. He didn't need to check his six. He knew his team had his back. He swept the ground floor and then led the advance up and out onto the rooftop. Movement to his left registered in his peripheral vision. Two pops followed by what sounded like a cough signaled that the sniper that had held them down was neutralized.

Fault Line©

Two members of the squad took up a defensive position. Bill and the other three men went back down the metal spiral staircase and met up with the other squad members. They conducted a quick sweep of the building on the other side of the courtyard. Nobody was home there either. That wasn't odd. Lots of people had left the city to avoid the fighting.

Bill had called the situation right. A pickup truck had blocked off the other end of the block. The back end of the truck was loaded down with enemy re-enforcements. The rest of the squad had taken up positions on both sides of the courtyard. If anyone tried to come in, they'd be caught in a crossfire. The broken door lying in the dirt gave away the presence of the first person to probe the entrance.

These guys were not all that bright. The gunfire stopped, signaling their approach. The door wobbled on its warped hinge.

The team was disciplined. They held their fire and waited for him to come further in, hoping more would be close behind. Once the insurgent saw them, he raised his weapon to fire. The team engaged with force taking out three men in the initial exchange. The enemy fell back and tossed a grenade over the wall.

The team had been expecting it and quickly threw it back over the wall. The sound of running boots preceded the blast.

The enemy tried two more assaults on their position and were repelled each time. They tried to surprise the soldiers by attacking them from the other side of the courtyard. The seasoned team had been prepared for that as well. It turned out to be a feint. Large caliber bullets started punching fist-sized holes through the wall by the downed door. They had gotten their hands on an M-60 machine gun or larger. Whatever it was it was passing through the wall like it was made of butter. The high caliber ammunition was coming from the western side of the alley, the direction where the pickup truck was. The men that were on the eastern side of the courtyard hit the ground, and low crawled out of the line of fire. Two men were down, and more had been injured from the shrapnel of the shredded wall.

"You and you," said Bill pointing to the two men nearest the stairs. "To the windows," he said pointing up. They responded as soldiers do in battle, they executed. There wasn't time for an acknowledgment.

Bill looked out of the window he'd taken position at. What he saw turned his guts into a tighter knot than they already were.

Daniel was lying in the dirt. He couldn't tell how bad he was hurt. The enemy was still firing. He watched his friend's leg jerk back from the impact. That was when he knew Daniel was gone. He hadn't cried out in pain. Nothing else moved except that leg.

Bill made himself turn his eyes back to the entryway to the courtyard. He was also looking at the front of the room they were in. It would only be a matter of seconds before they figured it out and started pouring fire in through the window and attempted to breach the door.

Bill's group was trapped. He knew more of the enemy would arrive soon. Where was the overwatch? A Blackhawk? An ex-fil team? Where was their damn support?

A Novel by T. L. Scott

The guys upstairs and on the roof must have been keeping them busy. That was the only reason Bill could think of why they hadn't come in yet.

More guns joined the fight. A lot more guns. From the sound of bodies falling outside their door, the enemy was not faring well. Re-enforcements must have arrived.

They came in hot and heavy, two squads closed on their location, fast. Minutes after they started it was over.

A jaunty knock to the rhythm of "A Shave and a Haircut, Two Bits" was followed by "Come out come out wherever you are. Come on guys, the coast is clear. We got you."

They picked up the wounded and dead and loaded them into a couple of Humvees. Those able to walk formed up with the Delta soldiers and fought their way back to the wire.

That was the first time he'd seen members of the elite Delta force in action. It was also the first time he met Raul and Sam. They fought side by side over the kilometer and a half route they took back to the wire. They came under fire the whole way. It was sporadic and disorganized and was also met quickly and lethally.

Fault Line©

It wasn't until he was changing out of his battle rattle that Bill discovered he'd been shot, twice. A clean through and through on the back of his left arm and as embarrassing as it was, in his right butt cheek. That piece of lead was still in there. The doc who removed it said that it had to have been from a ricochet or it would have done more damage as he was digging it out. Bill kept that slug as a memento. He wore it on a chain around his neck till the day he died.

He applied for the Delta program the next day. While it was being processed, he got to know and became friends with, Raul and Sam when they were between missions. They filled him in on what the teams were like and gave him tips to train for the rigorous demands of training for the elite Delta Teams.

They kept in touch after the deployment, and when Bill completed training and became a team member, he requested assignment to the same team. Someone must have looked out for him because he got it. He found out later that it wasn't uncommon for people to be assigned based on referrals. This wasn't to be confused with nepotism. This was all about getting a referred known quantity as a member of your team. It was always better to have someone on your team that a trusted member vouched for. It wasn't ever about liking the person. It was all about whether you were good enough to trust with their life. Bill was that good.

Bill sat back and watched the sparks from the fire climb higher into the night sky. He took a deep breath trying to center himself back at home. He could still smell the air, a mix of dust, herbs, dung, and sweat; always the sweat.

"You all right brother?" asked Raul.

"Yeah bro, just thinkin'," said Bill.

"You do that too much, too much thinking. You should take it easy more bro'," said Sam. He put his hands behind his head and flexed his powerful biceps. "I let these babies do the thinking for me."

Bill didn't even bother to respond. Sam liked to act like a big meathead, but the truth was that he was one of the smartest people Bill had ever known. He spoke four languages, could build, repair, and hack a computer so easily it was scary, and he was also a demolition expert. He was good to have on your side in a fight. The man didn't quit. None of these guys did. That was one of the things that set them apart from others, they didn't quit, and never on each other.

"You sure you're okay man?" Raul wasn't satisfied. He saw the worry on Bill's face. Raul had the biggest heart of them all. He was always looking out. If Bill were, to be honest with himself, he would say that as much as he loved these guys like the brothers they were, Raul was the one he felt closest to. He was the one he opened up to when something was on his mind. He was more than a mentor. He was his best friend. Everybody knew it, and nobody cared. They were brothers, and they had each other's backs.

They sat by the fire and watched the stars. Not once did anyone bring up what had happened that morning.

Bill's sister Julie and her fiancé, Tom, came by around nine-thirty. His parents had sat down in their rocking chairs and were holding hands, content to listen to the kids do the talking. It was a good night.

A Novel by T. L. Scott

Chapter 5

Bill woke up to the smell of coffee and fresh bacon and eggs before he opened his eyes to the day. Those were the smells of home. The smells he'd woken up to countless times over the past seven months, only to have them disappear once the fog of sleep cleared from his mind. Those smells, along with a multitude of other small, everyday things were what he held on to. They were the things that helped him to get through the pain, boredom, loneliness, and fear of being at war. Those small things were what he was fighting for. Those small things that made up everyday life. The small things that made life good.

The kitchen was buzzing with activity. The guys were already seated around the table talking about football.

"You're going to see man. This year the Giants are going to have a good team," said Raul.

"Not good enough to beat the Patriots though." Sam couldn't resist needling him. As he expected, that was enough to set Raul off.

"We're going to kill them, man. They cheat every chance they get. They can't win unless they cheat." He continued to rant. "The Eagles got their number though, didn't they bro?"

"Yeah, they did," said Sam. "I wouldn't count Brady out though. He'll be in the fight next year."

"Nah, he's done, man. I bet he retires," Raul said.

"I hate to say it but watch out for the Lions this season," declared Sam.

"I thought you were a Bears fan?" asked Bill.

"Yeah, I am. I have to be honest though, they aren't going to get more than six wins this year if they're lucky. That new quarterback should get better this year but ... And, as if all that wasn't enough, their defense is ranked as one of the worst in the league. They used to be known as one of the best defensive teams." Sam just shook his head.

"Don't worry brother, Tampa and Miami are both in rebuilding years too. I really don't expect much out of either of them."

"Okay Bill, go ahead and tell us how great Dallas is going to be this year," said Raul.

"Not so good," he answered. "Watch out for Houston though. With JJ Watt healthy watch out," he said nodding his head knowingly.

And to that, no one had anything more to say. They had plenty more to say about the Bears and the Giants though. The discussion lasted for another few minutes and when the voices began to grow louder Bill's mom stepped in.

"Now, now, gentlemen let's keep it to a dull roar. Tommy, is it? Be a dear and get the orange juice out of the fridge. The rest of you boys make yourselves useful and set the table. Bill how is the coffee?"

"Mom you know you make the best coffee in the world."

"Well, thank you for that. Now, let's see how well I taught you and make the next pot, it looks like it could use a refill." She was master of her domain and ran it with military precision. It was no wonder where Bill had learned his discipline from.

"Mom has dad already gone out to the field?"

"I don't think so. He said something about going to the barn for something or other. You know him. He can't even wait till he has a full belly before he takes on the day."

Fault Line©

"Say grace before eating," his mother commanded once they were all seated around the old wooden table again.

"Dear Lord, bless this food we have received from your grace and please, Lord, help these boys to keep each other safe. In your name, we pray. Amen," said Bill's Mom.

Like most homes, the kitchen was the room that tied everything together. Whenever Bill thought of home, it was invariably this room that came to mind. He thought back to all the times that he had worked on his homework after school while his mom prepared dinner. Sitting at this very table, he had learned to read, how to add and subtract. He had thought that he would go crazy trying to memorize his multiplication tables while his mother wouldn't miss a beat no matter how many questions he asked her. She had taught him things that were not in his text books while putting together dinner. She had helped him to understand how to make sense of Shakespeare and Dante right in this room. This was her domain, and she was in control of all that happened here.

In no time, the food was eaten and the table cleared. Bill insisted that they clean up after the meal. With military precision, the soldiers put the kitchen back in order as his mother relaxed at the table with a cup of coffee.

Once everything was done, the guys made their way out to the porch. On his way out the door, Bill paused and kissed his mother on her forehead. He noticed that there was more gray peppering her brown hair than the last time he'd been home. He decided that he liked it that way.

"Mom, I know I don't tell you enough. I love you. Thank you for everything. You and dad have given me a good life. When I'm over there, and I get to thinking about home, I see your face, and it always brings a smile to mine." He wrapped his arms around her and hugged her close.

She gently pushed him away and stood up on her toes to kiss his cheek. "Thank you, you're a good son." She put her loving hand on his cheek. "I'm very proud of the man you've become."

He looked at her upturned face until she broke the moment and stepped back from him. The tender moment had passed, she turned to go back to her coffee.

"Mom, I'm going to go out and see if dad could use a hand unless there's something I can help you with."

Fault Line©

"No son, go on now. After all this time I have my routine. Go spend some time with that old grump of a man. Remind him that we have company and I expect him home for dinner."

"Yes ma'am, I will," he said as he eased the screen door closed behind him. As a boy, he had learned his lesson about slamming the door. Funny how some lessons stayed learned Bill thought with a smile on his face.

He found his dad right where he thought he would, up to his elbows in the engine of the old John Deere. It was the old John Deere because the new one was parked outside the barn. The old John Deere had outlasted two newer models that had been traded in over the years. The old Deere had belonged to Grandpa Williams. The current project was replacing the seals on the engine. His dad took loving care of the old tractor. The most work the tractor saw nowadays was driving in the Thanksgiving parade. Sam was on the other side of the engine block, happily in his element.

Bill took up his usual place on the opposite side of the engine from his dad, this time standing next to his friend. They both knew this routine. Bill and Sam had both grown up in this environment. They worked well together. None of them was the type that needed to talk a lot. They limited their conversation to the task at hand. Long stretches of time passed when nothing needed to be said. None of the men felt the need to fill the empty space with small talk. These were working men. Their actions told their stories. Bill remembered that at times hours would pass and not more than ten words would pass between them. It was never a cold silence though. They were comfortable with each other.

"Where are the guys?" asked Bill.

"Helping Michael and Dave muck out the stalls," his father answered.

"I'm going to go and see if they need any help with those stalls," said Sam.

"I'm sure they're doing just fine. David can keep 'em in line. He isn't the brightest bulb, but when it comes to work nobody works harder than that boy does," said Bill's dad.

"All the same sir, I'm going to leave you two to it. Thank you for letting me work on her with you," he said patting the old tractor with his hand before jumping down to the dirt floor.

Fault Line©

Sam knew they needed some family time. He went out of the barn and just stood in the yard for a few minutes, taking in the scene around him. The air felt cleaner; somehow it was clear air. The air over in Afghanistan had always felt like it was dirty. Like there was a sandy residue in everything. The air at home in Virginia was different too. It was always humid. Here it felt crisp. He took a deep breath and held it for a couple of beats, just enjoying the sensations around him.

"Something's not right," said Bill's dad as he applied pressure to the torque wrench.

Bill knew that he needed to wait while his dad said what was on his mind. Years of experience had shown him that his father moved at his own pace.

"I've been thinking about what happened. It just don't feel right. I know son. Crazy things like this don't always make sense. This feels like something more than just a crazy guy losing it though. There's something about that woman that I keep coming back to. Something I can't quite put my finger on." His dad raised his eyes from the next bolt he had to tighten and looked at Bill. "Promise me you'll keep your eyes open."

A Novel by T. L. Scott

"I will dad." Bill knew that this was way out of character for his dad. He'd raised him to know what to do. He had taught him how to fight, how to hunt, how to shoot. He had taught him how to read people. How to watch their eyes for the truth. Not just the truth of what they were saying, but the truth of what they were going to do.

Bill knew his dad well enough that if this had him concerned enough that he felt he needed to say something, then he was really upset about it.

Bill had been thinking the same things as his dad. The difference was that he had not told his father, or the sheriff for that matter, everything. Some things he had held back. Like the look on the woman's face. She'd been afraid. That was to be expected. What Bill was surprised about is what he didn't see. He didn't see surprise. The more he went over it, the surer of it he became. He also kept thinking about that feeling he had that the sheriff was leaving out more than he knew. Of course, that was what he expected of the sheriff. But he hadn't seemed surprised either.

Fault Line©

Chapter 6

The dirty dishes from lunch had been cleared away, and everyone that wanted apple pie and ice cream had it in front of them. Julie gave her maid of honor Sara a little nod of the head.

Sara was a bundle of energy. She was one of those people that was always doing something. Somehow, she had become the go-to person for planning weddings. This would be the fifth wedding she had organized in the last two years. It seemed that all her friends were getting married. She joked that before much longer she would be the last woman standing.

"Okay, it has been a lot of work, but we are almost there," Sara began. "Father Sanchez called me this morning to say that he can make it. The stomach virus has passed, and he says his appetite is back with a vengeance." They all knew that the good Father had a large appetite and a correspondingly large stomach to show for it.

"We have Tony's reserved from six to nine. Tony told me that if we need longer, it's no problem. He said that he booked us for the whole night. If we finish early, he'll just flip the sign over." Tony's had the distinction of having the best pizza for miles around. Everyone knew that as soon as they finished, the place would fill up with customers in no time at all.

Sara talked about the seating arrangements for the dinner and what would be served. She then moved on to the seating arrangements at the church. She went over the layout of the church for Bill's friends' benefit. Everyone else knew it well. They had been going there for their whole lives. The new Church was over one hundred years old. In many ways, the town had grown around the Church. The current building had been built on the site of the original church. It had burned down when a bolt of lightning hit it during the big storm of 1911. The fire had also claimed three other buildings before the townspeople were able to get it under control.

"I still say you shouldn't invite your uncle Gavin. He'll only make trouble."

"Dad," said Julie, "I want Uncle Gavin to be there."

"He's a no-good drunk, and everyone knows it," said William.

Fault Line©

"Dad, Uncle Gavin will be fine. He's family, and he will be there, and you *will* get along with him." Julie gave her father her most disarming smile. The one he never could say no to. She had perfected that smile as a little girl and had only become better at it over the years. When she used it on her fiancé', he was putty in her hands. *Fiancé'?* That word still sounded so strange, and in only two days he would be her husband. *HUSBAND!!* Now that was a strange word! It was really happening. She was getting married. It still seemed like a dream at times. As strange as the word husband sounded, she knew that he was the right man for her.

"Listen to me," announced Julie. She raised her hands to get their attention. "All of you, please really listen to me now. I love you all. I really appreciate all the hard work you have put in to make this a great wedding. Everything has been planned. We even planned for contingencies. Something *will* go wrong. We *will* deal with it. You all know that. That is what we do. We deal with it and make the best out of whatever happens. I love you all, now take a deep breath," she said as she inhaled and raised her arms for all of them to follow her lead. "Now, exhale and relax, and let's have a good time. Hey! This is a Thompson and Camacho wedding, and somebody will either throw up on someone or pass out on the dance floor. We know that. We also know who is most likely to do it and can keep an eye on them. Dad," she said turning to her father "you always taught us to control the chaos as much as possible, and to deal with all else." She smiled at him lovingly, squeezed his hand, and then turned back to her assembled family and friends. She turned back to him. "Oh, and remember the other nugget of wisdom you taught us?" With a deep voice, she did a surprisingly good imitation of her father. "Even the best-laid plans are forfeit once the first shot is fired. Suck it up and deal with it!"

Everyone broke up into laughter as father and daughter hugged each other.

"I love him, daddy."

"I know you do, princess. I know you do."

"Where is Tom? I thought he was going to be here."

"You know how much he hates all this planning for the wedding stuff. I let him off the hook. He said that his dad wanted

to meet with him. He told him that it was important. He better
not be trying to tell him that something came up."

"Honey, he is a Senator and things do come up from time
to time."

"I know dad. But he always has things that come up and
take priority over Tom and his sister. This is something that he
has known about for a year. Unless we're under invasion, he
better not try to get out of this."

Looking at the fire in his daughter's eyes William knew
that the Senator was close to crossing a line he likely would not
be able to come back from. She was already defensive of the
neglect Tom had suffered growing up. She would not just sit by
and let it continue to happen. He knew from his own past
struggles that she had no fear to stand toe to toe when she knew
she was in the right. She almost always was too. Her moral
compass was as rigid as her mettle. She was just like her mother.

A Novel by T. L. Scott

Chapter 7

Bill, Sebastian, and Raul were out getting supplies for the bachelor party. They didn't plan on going crazy or anything, but every man deserved a good bachelor party. Plus, the more Bill thought about it, the more he liked the way that the idea of a bachelor party made his sister nervous. The way he figured it, it was good for a bride-to-be to be a little bit nervous about the groom. There should be some question about whether everything was going to work out as planned. It made the anticipation all the sweeter.

He wasn't planning on doing anything too crazy to Tom. It wasn't like he was going to get him drunk, throw him onto a train bound for Houston or anything. Plus, on the radio, they'd just said that the storm out in the Gulf had been upgraded. The forecasters were saying that hurricane Francesca might make landfall as early as tomorrow and if they were right, she had Houston in her sights. Of course, if that happened, Galveston would get the worst of it. That was the last thing Galveston needed. It still hadn't recovered from hurricane Beatrice. That one had been a category three. The problem was, Beatrice had stalled over the coast. It stayed in place for eighteen hours and churned up the storm surge to nineteen feet as well as dumping massive amounts of rain. The seawall had done what it could, but the surge was too big. With all of the rain that had already saturated everything on the small island, when the surge broke over the wall, Galveston was literally underwater. Houston was beat up pretty bad as well. There was serious flooding, but it was mostly from the rain and not the sea. That had been five weeks ago. Now another hurricane was feeding off the warm waters of the Gulf of Mexico, and this one was a monster. Francesca's winds had already been measured at 170 mph, and forecasters were predicting that to increase before making landfall.

"You see man?" said Raul "Now that's why I don't live on the coast. Hurricanes are nasty man. They are just so damn big. My cousin used to live in Florida when that hurricane hit a few years back. He was smart, and him and his family evacuated. When they came back, there was a tree in their living room, and only two walls were still standing. Do you want to know what was crazy though? The dog house in the backyard was good as new. Hurricanes are crazy man. Thank God we ain't on the coast."

Bill knew better than to say anything. He grew up here and knew that while they wouldn't get the brunt of the storm, they would feel it. Raul had said it: hurricanes are big and nasty. Even though they were hundreds of miles from Houston, they would still likely feel her wrath. Even though he knew that the storm was still a long way off, he couldn't stop his eyes from looking up at the sky. It was strange that it was a beautiful day with barely any clouds in the sky. If they were lucky, it would stay that way. The odds were that the storm would turn east once it made landfall and miss them completely. Most of the computer models the news people kept quoting said so. Only a couple of tracks had the storm dancing west before taking a sharp turn to the east. It would all depend on a low-pressure front moving in from the Rockies.

Bill's eye caught movement in an upstairs window of a house they were driving past. A little girl was looking out of her bedroom window, watching them as they were passing by. For some reason, he felt that she was very sad. Bill could tell that the girl was looking at him as well. The expression on her face didn't change. Whatever she had done to be in her room on such a beautiful day must have been bad, he reasoned. Well, that, or her parents were fucked up. God, I hope not! But Bill wasn't naïve. He knew there were a lot of kids who lived in Hell every day.

They found all the supplies they were looking for without needing to go to too many stores. In the process, Bill ran into people he hadn't seen in years. It was a small town, so he knew most of the people but some he didn't remember. Funny how time fades things, he thought with a mental shrug.

They stopped for lunch at Maria's. As far as Bill was concerned Maria's was the best food in town. He liked Tony's, but Maria put magic into her tacos and burritos. When it came to her chorizo, well, it brought you closer to heaven.

The guys were still used to being down-range and as such didn't talk much while eating. They were more focused on the food than making small talk. Bill was stuffing his face with his third taco when the bell above the door announced the entrance of another patron.

He recognized her at once. If anything, she was more beautiful than he remembered. That thought made him remember the half-eaten taco between his plate and mouth. *Oh Shit! Is there something on my mouth?* he thought as his other hand scrambled for a napkin.

Isabella made her way to a small table against the wall. Bill noticed that she sat with her back to the wall. Interesting, he thought to himself. A little smile played at the corner of her mouth as her eyes found his. She raised her hand and gave him a small wave. He gave one right back. The waitress must have thought that she was signaling her because she materialized beside her table to take her order.

While that was going on, Bill made short work of his remaining taco and found the bottom of his glass of iced tea. He was confused as to what to do next. He wanted to talk with her but didn't want to impose on her privacy. She was there to eat after all.

Fault Line©

"May I join you?" She asked, solving the problem for him. She was standing right beside his table and looking directly at him.

Raul, ever the ladies' man, was the first to answer her. "Well, of course, a pretty lady like you is welcome at our table."

Sebastian sprang up and pulled a chair out for her and swept his hand gallantly to the side. "My lady," he said with a small bow.

"Thank you," she said.

"Sebastian, ma'am."

"Thank you, Sebastian," she said with a big smile.

Once she was settled, Bill asked her how she'd been doing.

"Good," she declared.

When no one said anything, she added "well, pretty good, . . . most of the time."

"Is there anything we can do to help you?" asked Bill.

"No, no, you guys have been great. You literally saved my life. I'll never be able to thank you enough."

The guys knew well enough to not say anything to that. They didn't want to say anything that might demean her gratitude.

"Bill, right?" she asked him. When he nodded his head, she went on. "I remember you telling me that you guys were back here to attend your sister's wedding. She hasn't put it off because of this trouble has she?"

"No, I don't think anything would make her let Tom get away from her for one more day. She's set on going through with this."

"You don't approve of that?" she asked him.

"No, I don't see any reason why she shouldn't go ahead with her plans," he said quickly, shaking his head. "It's just that I don't think Tom knows yet how stubborn my sister is once she makes up her mind."

"Is that a family trait?" she asked him, giving him a bright smile that lit up her eyes.

He thought she was beautiful before. His assessment just got adjusted to stunning.

"I suppose it is," he said.

"Suppose?" asked Sebastian. "Bill here is one of the most stubborn guys I've ever met," he said as he leaned over and wrapped his arm around Bill's shoulder.

"You ain't kidding," added Raul. "When this mother. . . Excuse me. When this guy decides to do something, he's mister follow-through. It's one of the reasons I let him hang with my boys and me."

They all had a good laugh at that one.

It was plain that Isabella was sizing him up. Bill wondered if it was because she was interested in him or if it was for some other reason. He reflected on her choice of seating again. Some people would have chosen to have their backs to the other diners so they could enjoy a sense of privacy. Bill and his friends would never have done that. You wouldn't be able to see any trouble coming at you.

The more he watched Isabella he noticed that her eyes were scanning the room. Yeah, she was engaging with Bill and the guys, but her eyes were always moving. Bill recognized it for what it was. It was the same way with him and the guys. They were always looking for trouble. You never knew when or from where it was coming. You just knew that it *was* coming.

Out of the blue, Bill found himself asking if she had plans for later. He rushed on before he lost his nerve. "We're going to go out to *The Thorny Cactus* around eight. We have to set things up for the bachelor party and will stick around for a few drinks. Would you like to come along?"

"That sounds fun," she said. "But only if you agree to play me in a game of pool."

"You've got a deal ma'am," Bill readily agreed.

Bill, of course, would not let Isabella pay for her meal. "It's what a gentleman does," he explained. That brought a smile to her lovely face.

After the check was settled, they made plans for meeting later.

Bill waved as Isabella drove off in her Ford Focus.

"Man, you gotta tell me how you do that," said Raul. "I mean, I was sitting right there, looking all good, like I always do, and she didn't even look at me. I mean not that way. She only had eyes for you." He shook his head dejectedly. "Really, tell me.

How do you do it, bro'?" Raul asked. "It almost makes me want to give up hope." He looked up with a big smile. "I did say almost. Ladies watch out tonight."

"Oh, shut up man. You know you're going to go straight for the biggest girl in the place. You always do," said Sebastian.

"What? Big girls need lovin' too! Don't act like you don't know. I saw you when we were in Atlanta last year. You like your girls thick too," he said drawing a pear shape in the air with a distinctive swell at the bottom.

"Bro' there is a difference between thick and jiggly."

"Yeah bro' thick girls give you some bounce, but jiggly girls give you a ride that lasts *all night long,*" Raul stated as he made a do-me face and thrust his hips.

Laughing, the guys climbed into Bill's Explorer and headed back to the farm. Raul was still trying to educate them on the merits of healthy girls as he was now calling them.

A Novel by T. L. Scott

Chapter 8

Bill arrived at the hotel a few minutes early, as was his habit, to find Isabella already waiting for him. She had changed into a black pair of jeans with a white blouse. Her tanned skin really stood out. She had pulled up part of her hair and let the rest of it fall around her shoulders. Before he could get out of the truck and get the door for her, she had already jumped in. This was not a lady who waited around for others to do things for her.

"Ready for a night of fun with the locals?" Asked Bill.

"I really am. I've been cooped up for too long. I can't remember the last time I just went out and had fun."

"What has had you so cooped up, if you don't mind me asking?"

Fault Line©

"Oh, it's exciting stuff!" She said to him with a small grin on her lovely face. "I have been doing research for an article I'm writing."

"And what scintillating topic has brought you all the way to this little piece of paradise?" Bill asked her with a grin.

"I don't know about scintillating, but it is important. I'm researching how children of illegal immigrants are managing integration into small towns in the American Southwest," Isabella said.

"That does sound important. It can't be easy though. I wouldn't think that the parents of those children just open their doors and say to come on in to their illegal alien home."

"That is the hardest part," said Isabella. "Talking with the local police and the teachers at the school is the easy part. The people at social services are always an immense help too. I spend time where the families are. I try to earn their trust, but it's hard. They are always afraid of being sent back across the border."

Isabella had turned her body to the side, so she was looking right at Bill as he drove the truck. This made it very hard for him to concentrate on three things at once, listening to her tale, looking at how gorgeous she was, and keeping the truck on the road without hitting anything.

"These are good people Bill. All they want to do is earn a living and provide a good life for their families. The stories they tell, about what drove them to leave their homes, are utterly horrendous."

When Isabella didn't elaborate, Bill knew better than to interrupt. He figured she was going over some of those stories again in her mind. If she wanted to share them, then he would listen, but he knew better than to push her. If she needed to talk about them, she would.

"I suppose you can understand what some of these families have faced," said Isabella as she looked back at him. "Mexico isn't Afghanistan, but they are both war zones. They both have terrorists that are brutalizing the people that call those countries home."

Fault Line©

The parking lot of *The Thorny Cactus* was over half full of mostly pickup trucks. Bill found a spot on the outer edge and backed in. As he'd anticipated, as soon as they were parked Isabella climbed out. She was definitely an independent woman.

"Is it usually this busy at," she paused as she checked her watch, "only a little after eight on a Thursday?"

"Of course, it is," he said with a smile. "Everyone is here to see Gracie."

"And who, may I ask, is Gracie?"

Their boots crunched on the gravel as they walked across the parking lot. They could already hear the music coming from the bar. The music swelled when a couple opened the door and went in. Bill and Isabella were only half-way across the parking lot when the door closed, cutting the volume.

"Wow, that's some good soundproofing," she said.

Bill just nodded his head. "Gracie's probably the most popular lady around here," he told her. "I'm surprised you've been in town this long and haven't heard of her. She has quite the following. Teens literally fight for a chance to dance with her. Men step out on their wives for a chance to have a turn. Old men gaze at her with fondness and a little jealousy that their time has passed. Gracie is quite the lady, but in the end, she breaks all their hearts. She simply will not be tamed. She's quite the wild one when she wants to be." They arrived at the entrance to *The Thorny Cactus*. They felt the music pulsing through the walls.

Bouncers were stationed at each side of the entrance. Isabella didn't fail to notice that Bill greeted each man by name. Once they were inside, he leaned in towards her and raised his voice so he could be heard over the music. "I used to play football with those guys."

"What did you say," she asked, moving a little closer to him.

Fault Line©

He put his hand up to his mouth and leaned closer to her. His lips were almost touching the cup of her ear. She smelled like something fruity and flowery at the same time. He wasn't much of a perfume expert but, on her, it smelled real nice.

"I said, I used to play football with those two guys." He had lowered his voice to a more conversational tone since he was so close to her.

He pulled his head back a little to see if she had understood him. She nodded her head that she did, then put her hand on his shoulder and raised up on the balls of her feet, bringing her mouth close to his ear. He hoped she hadn't noticed the shiver that ran through him when she touched his shoulder.

"Do you know everybody in here?" she asked.

He raised his head and looked around the bar. Seeing his friend's sitting at a booth on the left side of the dance floor, he raised his hand to let them know he'd seen them.

A Novel by T. L. Scott

He lowered his head back to Isabella again. "Not everyone, just the interesting people." He smiled as he pulled away from her. "Come on," he said, tilting his head toward his friends.

They were settled into a booth near the room with the pool tables. Bill led her across the bar. He cut across the edge of the wooden dance floor which was mostly free of dancers. They were gathered closer to the stage, four deep, doing a line dance. Most of the people were either already on the dance floor, or they had staked their claim on a booth and weren't giving it up for the night. Over at the bar, the crowd was thickening. It was only two or three deep at the moment. In a little while, that would swell to much more. They made it to his friends with a minimum amount of jostling. A cold pitcher of beer and a pair of freshly filled glasses were waiting for them when they sat down.

"So, were you able to get the supplies?" asked Bill.

"Yeah, but you wouldn't believe how hard it was to find a tutu in that size," said Sam.

Fault Line©

"It's going to be so cool though. It was worth driving over to Greenburg for it," added Tommy.

"You're not going to believe what else we found," said Sam. He reached into a plastic bag he had beside him and pulled out a sparkly tiara. "This is the perfect touch with the tutu."

"Is this going to be a bachelor party or what?" asked Isabella.

"We're not going to get too crazy, but the first time he tries to call or text Julie he has to put on the tutu. The same if he answers a call or a text from her," explained Bill.

"Why don't you just take his phone at the beginning of the night?" she asked.

"Too easy," answered Raul. "He has to control himself. He's also got to show her that she can trust him. He doesn't have to jump just because she reaches out to him. There will be times that he is busy and will have to get back to her later."

"Yeah, but the real reason is that we will get to show the pictures during the wedding reception of him wearing a tutu and a tiara. Oh, the sweet memories," exclaimed Sebastian.

Bill took a couple of drinks from his beer while they caught each other up on what they had been doing. After a little bit, he excused himself. "I have to go talk with the owner for a few minutes. I'll be right back," he said looking right at Isabella. He made eye contact with his friends and gave a little nod of his head before walking away from them.

"So, what brought you to this lovely town Bill likes to call home?" asked Sebastian.

"I'm a journalist," she explained. "I've been running down a story about migrant workers. It's a tough life for the workers in the field. I'm trying to tell the story about the families. Show the struggles they go through as they bounce across our country. It's a story about America that most people don't know but should."

"Sounds interesting," agreed Sebastian. The other guys were nodding their heads in agreement.

"So, how about you guys? Did you all grow up around here?" she asked.

They each told her their story of where they had come from and why they had joined the Army. Sam was the last one to go so as he was wrapping up he asked her where she had grown up.

"I grew up in a small town outside of Phoenix. Dad was an accountant and mom taught second grade. It was a pretty normal childhood, boring, but normal."

"So why are you chasing down this story here?" asked Sebastian.

"I've worked hard to get close to this family. It's taken me three months to gain the mother's trust enough for her to allow me in. They are all afraid that they'll get reported and end up being deported back to Mexico. With all the talk by the politicians, it has become a very hostile environment to be from Mexico. It was never easy for them, but now there are real problems. You wouldn't believe the violence that goes on against them, and the police don't do anything to protect them. If they do end up getting sent back to Mexico, it's even worse. You wouldn't believe some of the horror stories I've been told of what's happening there. Those gangs are merciless. Whole families have been slaughtered. I'm sure you heard about that family that was murdered at a wedding. Their decapitated heads were left on display as a warning. These people are pure animals."

The conversation waned after that. Each person was lost inside their heads, reflecting on the tragedies they had witnessed.

Isabella looked around the room and saw the typical crowd. People just out to have a good time with friends. The dance floor was busy but not crowded yet. The dancers were moving to a line dance. More people were joining the fun as she watched.

Her eyes fell on a group of men across the room. Something about them had arrested her attention. She only had a fleeting look at them as the crowd ebbed and flowed across the dance floor. The small looks she was able to get, in between the swirling skirts and tight jeans, confirmed that the men that had caught her attention stood out from the rest. They were a rough looking bunch. That wasn't it though. There were other rough looking groups here. It was their attitude she had noticed. They were leaning in towards each other, obviously engaged in their conversation. The men around them were look outs. That was what had caught her attention. Over time, Isabella had learned to pick up on these minute details. Two men were standing to each side of the table, their backs to the four seated men. They were actively scanning the room. Their eyes were always on the move, heads slowly rotating as they assessed the crowd.

"So, you noticed our friends too," said Bill, startling her out of her thoughts. He slid back into his spot in the booth across from her.

She thought about playing it off but immediately discarded the idea. Bill would know it to be a lie and she didn't want to lie to him.

"They don't really blend in do they?" she asked.

"No, they don't. Do any of them look familiar to you?"

Isabella turned and looked at Bill. "No, why would they?"

"Well, I have a feeling they are tied in with that guy that you had a disagreement with the other day."

"A disagreement?" she asked raising her left eyebrow.

"Yeah, he wanted to hurt you, and you weren't agreeing to it."

"I guess that's one way of looking at what happened." He really liked the way she smiled.

Bill was wondering where this mysterious woman had picked up her crowd spotting skills. It was possible that she was just good at reading the situation. He knew that some people were more in tune than others. He somehow doubted that it was anything that simple. There was definitely more to this stunning beauty.

He let his eyes drift over the crowd some more. The bar still had some room at it. Three bartenders were keeping up with the crowd. He knew that there would be two more who would start working soon. Things were about to pick up. He continued to pan his gaze to the right and saw that Sam and Tommy were playing for one of the pool tables. *The Thorny Cactus* had six tables that were in decent enough shape. They were always good for drawing some action. Tonight would surely be no different. It was a given that some fights would break out. The staff was quick to respond and hustle it out to the parking lot. Once there, they usually stood by and let them work it out. They only stepped in when it was apparent they were needed. Most of the people who came to *The Thorny Cactus* were regulars. In fact, most of the fighters were regulars too. Regular to get into a fight at least. Bill had danced a couple of times out in the parking lot himself. *"Ah, the fond memories*, he thought to himself."

Bill was surprised when he felt Isabella grab his hand.

"Come on; this lady needs to dance."

Ever the gentleman Bill could only oblige the lady. He was grateful. Not only did he get the chance to dance with the best-looking woman in the place, it would also give him the opportunity to get a better look at the guys he had spotted earlier.

The band was doing a good cover of the Sara Evans song "Suds in the Bucket" and the dancers were kicking up the sawdust on the floor. Bill was pleasantly surprised at how good the band sounded. They were local, and he knew most of them had been playing together for years.

The lead singer was new though. She had a smooth voice and could really hit the notes. He remembered her as being a shy girl in school. That shy girl was not the woman up on the stage now.

Fault Line©

Bill looked into the mirror behind the bar and saw the group he'd been looking for. He split his attention on spinning the lovely lady he was dancing with and the group of men sitting over in the corner by the pool tables.

"Are they doing anything suspicious?" Isabella asked him.

"Define suspicious." He kept the smile on his face as he looked into her beautiful brown eyes. "I don't know why but they feel wrong." In truth, Bill knew what had set him off. They were set up in a defensive posture like they were expecting trouble. By the look of this group it was likely they planned to cause some trouble of their own.

The band shifted into a slow song. Bill looked at Isabella to make sure it was okay with her if they kept dancing. She smiled up at him and wrapped her arms around his waist, drawing him into her embrace. Bill felt his heart trip over itself, and then it began to race.

"Look at that lucky mother fucker," said Raul. "Somehow he always ends up with the ladies."

"Oh, shut up, you jealous son of a bitch. You know Bill ain't been with nobody," replied Sebastian. "You're just mad it isn't you out there dancing with her." Tommy topped up both of their mugs from the pitcher. "A toast," he proposed, raising his mug, "to ladies we'll never have and good beer that we will."

Both Bill and Isabella split their attention between dancing and watching the group of men. Four men were sitting at the table and two standing, keeping guard. Bill realized he might have missed more of the group. He let his eyes scan the room. This was something he'd been trained for. It wasn't any different than in the war zone. Most of the people were exactly what they appeared to be. Normal people, living their lives and trying to have a little bit of fun along the way. It was the other people that he was looking for. Once you knew what to look for they stood out from the crowd.

Bills eyes fell on a big man. He was about 6'4" and weighed at least 250 pounds of what looked to be mostly muscle. The set of his face made his rough appearance look aggressive. He looked like a pit bull about to launch into a fight. He really stood out from the crowd. Now that he had keyed onto the man Bill imagined the anger pouring off him. Bill followed the man's gaze and knew that he wasn't part of the group he was concerned about. The man was looking at one woman in particular. She was a pretty brunette with a nice figure out on the dance floor. She was dancing slowly with a man, their hands caressing each other. It looked like they were a couple. It was obvious that the big man didn't have good intentions on his mind. Maybe he was an ex-lover that she had spurned. Maybe she had turned him down for a dance, and he was a real hot-head. He mentally marked where the man and the couple were in the bar. If things heated up, he liked to know as much about the situation as possible.

Bill let his eyes continue to wander and found two men, one on each side of the entrance. Their eyes were scanning the crowd. The other people moved around these two men. They were like boulders in a river, and the people were like the current flowing around them. They were not blending in.

"What's going on Bill?"

The dancers, as well as most of the other people in the bar, were moving towards an area on the opposite side from the pool tables.

"I believe it's time for Gracie to start her dance. They are literally going to be waiting in line for a turn with her."

"Bill, I have to let you know right now that I don't swing that way. Watching some stripper is not my idea of a good time."

"Come on Isabella. I think you'll really like this," said Bill as he cut a path for them through the crowd.

Gracie already had her first dance partner. She was taking it easy on him. Nice and slow to start.

"So, she's Gracie?" asked Isabella. "I have to say she's not what I was expecting."

"What? Didn't I describe her good enough?

Fault Line©

"Well, I thought she would be a little taller," Isabella said with a smile.

They watched the first rider try to stay on while Gracie picked up the pace and started to buck and twist with more energy. The crowd was cheering the rider on. He actually did pretty well, in Bill's opinion. In the end, Gracie threw him. The crowd cheered his efforts and helped to pick him up. The next challenger was a young woman. She climbed up on the mechanical bull, got settled in, and with her free hand slapped the rawhide. "Alright Gracie, you bitch! Let's dance!" The crowd roared its approval as Gracie started her dance.

Bill looked behind him to check on his friends. The booth was empty. That was strange. One of the guys should've been there. They wouldn't give up the booth. He looked over at the pool tables. Seeing what was going on, he shot out his hand and took Isabella by hers. He pushed his way back through the crowd. He picked up the pace when he saw what was going on. As they made their way past the table with the hard-cases, Bill made eye contact with one of the two men still sitting there. They only looked at each other for a second, but they both knew that they had made each other.

Bill and Isabella continued to the pool room. They saw that Sam and Sebastian were fully engaged with four thugs. Bill saw two more lying on the floor. He stopped short of entering the room when he saw that Tommy and Raul were already there. They were standing by in case they were needed. Bill relaxed and turned to find one of the men from the table walking up to him. He stopped advancing when Bill turned. They stood there looking at each other. Neither one backing down. Bill protectively moved Isabella to the side.

The man facing Bill let a smirk crease his scarred face. It was apparent that he had battled acne in his youth. His smile turned to a sneer when Bill didn't advance on him. The man didn't make a move towards Bill either.

Fault Line©

The other man from the table put a hand on his friend's shoulder and said something to him. They both turned and went back to their table.

Bill turned his attention back to his friends. The odds were now fair as two more bad guys were on the floor and the last two were soon to follow. The bouncers finally showed up and put an end to the fight. They escorted the six guys that had started the fight out of the bar.

Sam filled them in on what had happened once they were settled back into their booth. "This guy went to walk around me and bumped my shooting arm on purpose. He was looking for a fight. He didn't even say anything before he threw a punch."

"Did you even feel that pool stick the other guy broke across your back?" asked Tommy.

"Hell yes!"

Sam looked up at Isabella. "Sorry, Isabella. "Yeah, I felt it, man. He hit me with the thick end."

"Well he didn't do so well after I hit him with a pool ball upside his head," said Sebastian.

"I take it he was one of the two I saw laying on the floor," said Bill.

"Yeah, his friend that started it joined him there. It was a good thing too because when I looked up, four more guys had come in to join in the fun."

"I don't think this was a simple disagreement guys. This whole thing feels like it was set up."

"Why didn't you guys join in?" Sam asked looking at Tommy.

"You were having so much fun," he said shrugging his big shoulders. "It would've been a shame to intrude," said Tommy.

"Gentlemen, excuse me," said one of the bouncers, "you'll have to leave as well. "Bill, I'm sorry but it's policy. All fighters have to leave for the night."

"We understand Steve. Thanks for giving us a few minutes for the other guys to clear out."

"Yeah, we watched them go before we came back in to talk with you."

"Can we finish our beers," asked Sebastian.

Steve made a point of looking at their glasses. "As soon as those are done, so are you guys, okay?"

"Thanks, Steve," said Bill.

Across the room, a nondescript couple quietly finished their drinks and then left the bar.

"Listen, guys, you know that we may step out into trouble," said Bill.

"But, the bouncer said that he saw them leave, right?" asked Isabella.

"Yeah, that's what he said," Tommy agreed.

"I'm sure they did leave. They're probably long gone, but it never hurts to be ready, just in case," Bill explained.

Isabella looked around at the men's faces and knew that they were expecting trouble. They didn't waste time drinking the rest of their beer. Raul stood and took the lead with Tommy close behind him. Isabella and Bill followed them to the door with Sam and Sebastian covering their rear. When they reached the exit, she noted that they quickly went through the door and then fanned out once they were clear. They kept their backs to the bar as they scanned the parking. Although she didn't see anything that looked out of the ordinary the men around her didn't relax their attitudes.

"Well," said Raul, "at least it wasn't a boring evening. I was worried, Bill, when you invited us to this little town of yours, that I would die from boredom."

Bill smiled at his friend. "I'm glad you're enjoying yourself. Listen guys; the rehearsal dinner is tomorrow at five. After that, we're going to have the bachelor party. Try not to get yourselves locked up between now and then," he said.

The group split up and went to their cars. Isabella was walking behind Bill a couple of steps heading towards his truck when he suddenly stopped.

"What is it?" she asked stopping just short of bumping into him.

Fault Line©

He reached his hand out, fingers splayed, signaling her to hold still. He was trying to find what had made him pause. Something was *off*. He strained to hear anything that was amiss. Something was out there, somewhere just beyond his senses. He was sure of it. He had quit questioning his instincts long ago. He strained to see anything that was off. Even something as simple as a leaf that was moving when it shouldn't be.

At the same moment, about fifteen feet into the trees a fierce set of eyes watched Bill's every movement. He knew his men wouldn't make a move unless he told them to. They hadn't made any noise to give their position away. The man had sensed that they were there. He knew he was watching a trained soldier. This was inconvenient. He noted that the man's friends hadn't left him. They had all been heading back to their vehicles. When they realized that their friend had stopped, they had spread out. Most people would have called out to their friend asking what was wrong. A few others would have walked over to join their friend and look at the same place. This group had spread out. He knew it was to minimize themselves as potential targets and also to cover more angles if they needed to.

The man had seen enough. He held his men in place until this group left. They then melted back into the darkness.

Two others had seen the whole thing. They had sat in their car and watched as the events had unfolded.

"What do you make of it, Mike?"

"I think we have a lot of players in this small town. It sure looked to me like they were testing each other."

"What? You think those guys circled back and waited for them to come out of the bar? That doesn't make sense. If they went to the trouble to lay a trap for them why didn't they spring it?"

"First of all, we don't know if the guys in the woods were the same as the ones that were in the fight earlier. It could have been them, or maybe the guys from the house were there. What I'm really worried about is that this whole thing was set up as a probe. If that was the case, then we're dealing with two groups of trained soldiers." He already knew that the man that had stopped short of his truck and his friends were almost certainly soldiers, probably Delta, or Marines. It was obvious that they knew what they were doing. It was also clear during the fight that they hadn't started it but sure knew how to handle themselves once in it.

FBI Special Agent Mike Cavanaugh made a call on his cell phone. "Any more activity," he asked once the line was connected.

"I haven't seen them come back yet."

"Okay, you know what to do." He hung up the phone and then started the Escalade.

"How do you feel about a late-night drive?" he asked looking at his partner.

"Sounds romantic. Summer is still in the air, the moon is shining bright, you picked me up in this nice ride, and you are such a gentleman. How could a girl say no?" she responded batting her long eyelashes at him.

A Novel by T. L. Scott

They both knew it for the joke it was. FBI Special Agent Kat Simmons was happily married to a beautiful woman that she loved very much.

Mike eased the big Cadillac out of the parking lot and onto state road 40. He turned north and followed the tail lights glowing in the distance.

Chapter 9

Isabella twisted in the passenger seat and looked at Bill. "So, are you going to tell me what happened back there?"

"I'm not sure," he said, still deep in his own thoughts.

"I believe that you don't know for sure what caught your attention. I don't believe that you aren't sure what it was though. Bill, I saw the way you stopped. It wasn't like something had been bothering you, and you stopped to puzzle it out. Something caught your attention, and it felt wrong to you. To be honest, I don't know if I was spooked by the way you were acting or if I felt something too, but it felt like we were being watched."

Bill turned his head and looked at her. "Keep going. You're right so far," he said nodding his head. He was intrigued with how perceptive she was. He also was trying to figure out this woman. She was beyond intriguing.

That kind of confused her and her face showed it. "Well, okay, the part that I can't figure out is, if it was the men from the bar hiding in the trees, then why didn't they come out to finish the fight?" She watched Bill nod his head in agreement, so she continued. "Why go to all the trouble to hide in the woods and then do nothing?"

"That's the right question," he said. "Why did they hold back?" Bill asked her. "The bouncers were in the bar. There were only a couple of other people in the parking lot. There was no reason for them not to finish the fight." Bill had already figured out that things didn't add up. The more he thought about it, the more he believed that the whole thing had been a set-up. He kept going back to the crazy man in the middle of Main Street. He knew the two events were tied together. He just didn't know how, yet. That brought him to the lovely woman sitting on the seat next to him. Who was this raven-haired beauty and how was she connected to all of this? Coincidence? Maybe. Then again, maybe not.

Bill eased up on the gas when he saw the brake lights of Raul's truck light up. He pulled over to the side of the road and coasted up next to him. He rolled down the window on Isabella's side of the truck as he pulled to a stop alongside his friend's.

"What do you want to do ,Bill?" asked Sebastian who was riding *shotgun* in the other truck.

"Let's just sit here for a minute and see what happens," said Bill.

Isabella looked at him. "Do you think we're being followed?" she asked as she craned her neck to look behind them.

"Bill, I see a car coming."

"Relax, this is a pretty busy road. It could be anyone." In-spite-of his words, he could feel the tension in both vehicles increase as the car got closer to them.

The light from the approaching vehicles headlights flooded both vehicles the closer it got. Bill had his foot on the brake, so he knew the car saw his taillights clearly.

At what seemed the last minute, the car signaled and went around them without slowing down.

"See, nothing to worry about," he said as he visibly relaxed. "Are you guys planning on going out again?"

Raul turned back to talk with the other guys. "No, it's probably a good time to call it a night."

"Isabella don't take this the wrong way, but I'd feel better if you stayed at my parent's ranch with us. I don't like the idea of you alone in your hotel room. I'm probably being paranoid, and I realize you don't even know me or anything but," Isabella stopped him by raising her hand like she wanted to ask a question.

"Will your parents be okay with this?" She asked him.

"Yeah, they'll be fine. I think you'll like them," he said. Satisfied with the smile Isabella gave him he turned his attention back to the other vehicle.

"Alright guys let's go back to the ranch.

About two miles down the road, Special Agent Simmons, Katherine to a few, and Kat to Mike was on the phone with the rest of the team.

"Any change, Tom?... So, they haven't come back yet?... Alright but save me a piece of that pizza. I don't care if it's cold. That's why God created the microwave." She hung up the phone and turned to Mike.

"No action at either house. What do you think's going on? This is strange."

"I agree," he said. "There are a couple more things I want to check out," he said, turning off the highway and onto a dirt two-track.

"Are you sure about this, Mike?"

"What? You said it was a romantic night with summer in the air and the moon shining brightly. Don't you want to go for an evening stroll on such a nice night?"

"You sure do know how to talk to a lady Mike Cavanaugh," she said as she flashed him a bright smile.

Mike and Kat had been partners on many ops like this before. They worked well together and trusted each other completely.

A few hundred yards down the road Mike pulled the car off to the side, hiding it behind a copse of trees he'd spotted a couple of days ago when they'd come out here for a recon run. Their destination was about two and a half miles to the east, as the crow flies. After checking to make sure they had what they needed, they set off across the scrub at an easy run. Twenty minutes later they were looking down on a long building that looked like it had once been a factory of some sort.

There were a lot of cars for this time of night. Mike counted four trucks and three cars that he could see. Lights were on at the north end of the building. A flash of light caused both of them to duck down. After a second Mike cursed "Damn! They've got sentries posted." He pointed to his left, at the nine o'clock position, relative to their current location. "It looks like that one is posted by the entrance road."

"Makes sense," agreed Kat. "They'd want to be warned of any cars approaching." She slowly looked over the ridge again.

Mike felt her tapping him on the arm to get his attention. She was pointing at a car coming down the road. Its lights were turned off to avoid attracting attention.

"Somebody coming to the party late?" She wondered aloud.

They watched as the car came around the last turn. It was a police car. "Oh shit," exclaimed Mike. "Either this cop is about to be killed, or we have one very dirty pig." The tension in his voice was clear. Kat knew that he was ready to jump into a firefight if needed. She knew that they couldn't if it came down to it. They were outgunned and not able to respond quickly enough to save this cops life if it came down to that.

"Damn, Damn, Damn!" he cursed as the car pulled in behind the building. He strained to hear anything, dreading the thought of shots breaking the stillness of the night. When the silence stretched past a minute, and then two, they allowed themselves to relax a little.

"Okay, so it's a dirty cop, and we don't know who it is."

"We could move to get a better look when he comes out," said Kat as she looked to their left. "The problem is we don't know if that's the only look-out. There could be more. Plus, with this bright moon, we don't have much cover."

He agreed with her. "So, we stay here and see what we see."

Fault Line©

Chapter 10

Everyone was in the kitchen enjoying another wonderful breakfast when there was a knock on the back door. Bill looked up to see the sheriff standing on the porch.

Bill's dad had been refreshing his cup of coffee, so he was closest to the door. He stepped over and opened it up. "Come on in, Sheriff. Want a cup of coffee?"

"Don't mind if I do." He looked at Bill's mom and nodded his head in greeting. "Ma'am, sorry for disturbing your breakfast."

She gave him a small, courteous smile.

"So, did you come by just for some of Maria's coffee?" asked Bill's dad.

"I wish it was that simple." He looked at the guys around the kitchen and noted the cuts and bruises. "I've been talking with the owner of *The Thorny Cactus* about the fight last night. I want to hear about it from you boys."

"Since you came out by yourself I assume you just want to talk. You don't want to bring them to the station, do you?" asked Bill's dad.

"No, of course not. Everyone agrees, they were just defending themselves. I wouldn't be here over a simple bar fight except some things don't quite fit." He looked at Bill. "I don't like it when things don't fit."

Bill nodded his head.

Sebastian took the lead and filled the sheriff in on what had happened inside the bar. When he was done, the sheriff stopped taking notes and looked up at him. Sebastian didn't add anything more, so he looked at the rest of the guys. When no one continued the story, he focused on Bill. "So, what happened next?"

"The bouncers came over to our booth and asked us to leave, after we finished our beers. We did, and then we did."

Again, the sheriff looked at each of the young men. No one volunteered anything more. "So, nothing happened out in the parking lot?" he asked.

"No Sheriff, nothing happened out in the parking lot. We got into our trucks, and we left. Simple as that." Bill explained.

"Simple as that, huh?" asked the sheriff with a doubtful look, keeping his gaze on Bill. After a good thirty seconds had passed, he took a deep breath and let it out slowly. "Okay then," he said as he looked down at his boots.

He collected his thoughts for a moment. Still looking at his boots, he asked another question. "Bill, why did you stop before getting into your truck? I talked with some of the people that were out there when you left. They said you just stopped and stood there looking into the woods."

He looked around at the young men, taking the measure of each, in turn.

"They also said that the rest of you spread out from each other. They said they didn't understand why you would all be looking in different directions. They reported that Bill was standing by his truck and they didn't know why none of you approached him to ask why he was just standing there."

He paused and let the silence hang for a minute. When no one volunteered an explanation, he continued. "They then said you guys just got into your trucks and left." He looked around the room and let his gaze fall on Bill again. "So, tell me, Bill, why did you stop before getting into your truck?"

"I thought I heard something," he replied.

Sheriff Olsen waited for more. When nothing came, he asked, "so was there something there?"

Bill looked the sheriff in the eye and without hesitation, answered him. "Yeah, I believe there was."

Again, the sheriff waited him out.

"There was someone, maybe more than one, out there. We were being watched. I'm sure of it."

Fault Line©

Sheriff Olsen knew better than to ask how he could have known that. He was an old Marine and had seen action himself. He trusted his instincts. Right now, they were telling him that these boys were telling the truth. He believed that there were probably men in the woods watching Bill and his friends. He even believed it was the men that had started the fight.

It made sense to lay a trap and wait for Bill and his friends to come out. It didn't make sense not to spring it. There weren't too many witnesses. None of his police officers were there to spoil their plans. It didn't add up to the typical bar fight scenario. He had a strong feeling that there was more going on than what he was seeing.

"Bill, would you mind coming down to the station?" he asked.

"Relax everybody," he said as he saw that everyone in the room had immediately tensed up. He looked back at Bill.

"You saw the man that was sitting at the table in the bar. The way you all told the story, he sounds like he was the leader of this group. You got a good look at him. I'd like you to come and take a look at some photos of people of interest and see if he comes up."

He shifted his gaze to Isabella. "Ma'am, I would like you to come as well."

"Sheriff, I already looked at those pictures, and nobody looks familiar," she said.

Sheriff Olsen nodded his head. "Yes ma'am, this is routine procedure. Sometimes, after a couple of days, the mind has a way of filtering through things, and people remember things they didn't before."

"Okay, but I don't think I'll be much help," she said.

Bill's dad stepped up to Sheriff Olsen and held out the pot of coffee. "One more for the road while they finish their breakfast?"

"That sounds good. Thank you, William." He turned and looked at Bill's mom. "I apologize for interrupting your breakfast, Maria. You do make the best coffee though," he said with a smile.

Fault Line©

Chapter 11

Cars kept showing up. Mike made the count at twelve, so far. Each of the guests had arrived with their *dad*. The tech team had alerted them to this potential party. Good police work, along with great technology, led to the arrest of seven men. The threads from their chat sessions showed their desire to meet with under-age girls.

They set up a fake meet with the girl from the chat. The girl was a member of the task force. She was petite and looked young. The house was wired to record everything from approach to final apprehension.

All of the men professed their innocence at first. When they were confronted with the actual history from their messaging, three admitted their intentions. One of the men insisted that all he wanted to do was to talk to the girl and convince her to stop talking to strangers so provocatively. All he wanted to do was to protect her, he claimed. The alcohol and condoms recovered from his car told a different story. It was the gift-wrapped lingerie with the fake name of the girl on the chat board that put a bow on his case. Knowing he was caught, he gave up the information on the secret party that was being scheduled.

Once the investigators knew where to look, they monitored the activity on the boards, while lurking in the background. They also pulled the past history and cast out their spiders to pull the threads on this organization. They watched as the "invitations" to the party were sent out last night to a select few members. Their history and backgrounds were combed through, and their accounts were scrubbed. The tech team continued to work their virtual ninja mojo while their identities were revealed to those in the field. Pictures were distributed to the field, and the security net dropped from the virtual net to the real world. It just so happened that the address was the same house Mike and his team had been watching for the past week. The authorization for the raid and all of the beaurocratic paperwork, to include the search and seizure warrant were expedited through, and the team was on stand-by.

Kat was taking the baby for a walk while Jim and Gabe were checking radio and electronic communications including the chatter on the dark web. Mike was on the scope. It was set up on a tripod that sat back from the window. The blinds were down in the room and turned to just a small opening. The eye of the scope had a non-reflective lens attached to avoid giving away their position with any flashes from the lens. In addition, they had set up two cameras with rotating optics at either side of the house. The feed was displayed in color on the laptop sitting on a table next to the tripod.

"How you doing, Kat?"

"It's a beautiful day for a walk honey. Don't you love it when mommy takes you out for a walk?" There was a pause. "Okay, sorry about that. There was a woman walking her Pomeranian. I'm not sure who looked more pompous, the dog or her."

"I'm about forty feet from the turn onto Dakota," she reported in.

"Be careful Kat. There's a lot of traffic arriving today, so they probably have spotters out. Keep your head down."

"Will do boss. I know you're watching my back."

That brought a smile to both of their faces. It was an inside joke of theirs. She always teased him about checking out her ass.

The morning sun was shining down from a cloudless sky. A small breeze was coming out of the west, so it was blowing towards her. When she turned onto Dakota Avenue, in another thirty feet, she would lose the breeze. Fortunately, there were some nice trees along the street to provide shelter from the sun. It felt good to be out of the house. She'd always been an athlete, and if she sat around too long, her legs started to get a nervous itch to them. She not only liked to run, she needed to. When she was on an op, she made-do, given the circumstances. For now, a steady walk would have to suffice.

The traffic on Sugarwood was steady. It was the main road that fed this development. When she turned onto Dakota, she knew there would be much less traffic. Dakota didn't lead into a cul-de-sac, but it wasn't a main thoroughfare either.

"Kat be careful. A couple of guys just came out of the house."

"Okay, got it. I'm making the turn."

The target house was the fourth one on the side of the street that Kat was turning the corner onto. They'd been surveilling it for the past week and a half. It was a nondescript two story with a brick façade. It blended in with the other nondescript homes that lined this nondescript street. In fact, this whole town was so normal she had a hard time remembering which *normal* town they were in. The people she hunted hid in the everyday normalcy of small-town America. They counted on people to accept a friendly face and depended on their accepting attitudes. With the low crime rates, people didn't have their guard up like they did in larger cities.

Since they'd been here, they had also picked up strange activity from a house on the other side of the street and two doors down. They believed they were using this place as a look-out post, providing security for the target house.

Two stood in the front yard of the one they referred to as the surveillance house, talking with each other. Kat knew from her training that these guys weren't just talking about the weather. Their positioning revealed their real purpose was to watch both approach angles. The fact that they were out of the house had brought her instincts up to full alert. She assumed they were expecting someone to arrive and were there to provide security.

From his vantage point in the house across the street, Mike saw Kat pushing the stroller around the corner. The thugs immediately picked her up. The taller of the two, the one that had been looking in her direction, broke away from his partner and started to cross the street. He had to stop and wait for a red Honda to drive past.

Kat picked him up as soon as he made his move. She stopped pushing the stroller and made a show of tending to her baby. She adjusted the baby blanket and acted like she put the pacifier back in the baby's mouth before resuming her morning walk. She was back in motion before the guy reached the curb ten feet in front of her.

She angled the stroller to the right of the sidewalk and put a half-hearted smile on her face as she closed the distance to the man.

He surprised her by stepping partially in front her.

She stopped and pulled the stroller protectively back, allowing a surprised look to take over her face.

He was a big man, well over six-feet-tall with an obviously muscular build. "Oh, I'm sorry ma'am. I didn't mean to startle you. I was wondering if you could help me. I'm new here and was wondering if you could tell me where there's a good place to get a steak around here."

"No, I'm afraid not," she said. "My husband and I are vegetarians."

She put her head down and aimed the stroller to her left, trying to get past him and be on her way.

He stepped into her path again and bent over to look into the stroller.

Kat jerked the stroller back from the man. "What do you think you're doing?" she demanded, raising her voice up an octave. She made a point of looking at a Prius as it drove past them.

"I'm sorry ma'am. I didn't mean to worry you," he said as he stood back up to his full height. "I just really like children."

Yeah, I know you do, you sick fuck, she thought to herself as she forced a half-hearted smile onto her face again. "There's a nice seafood place about two miles from here on Greenway," she told him. "It isn't steak, but it's a nice place. I hope that helps," she said to him, nodding her head and smiling at him to signal the end of their tet-a-tet.

He again blocked her path when she tried to go around him. "I thought you said you were a vegetarian. I didn't think vegetarians ate meat. Fish is meat, isn't it?"

She forced a put-upon smile on her face. "We don't eat red meat. We have fish sometimes though. The restaurant's name is *The Bayou.* They specialize in Creole style cooking. Now, if you'll excuse me, I need to be going."

He reached out his meaty hand and grabbed the end of the stroller and bent down to look inside. "I just want to look at this beautiful baby. With a good-looking mother like you, I'm sure he's a real cutie," he said leering at her.

She tried to jerk the stroller back from him, but he held firm to the bar on the front. She looked up and down the street and didn't see any help coming her way. The only person she saw was the other look-out who was still standing across the street. She was only seconds from her cover being blown. Hoping to salvage the situation she pulled out her can of mace.

"Get away from my baby, or I'll spray this." She said in a shaky voice that she hoped came across as scared yet protective.

His hand reached around towards his back. Reacting without thinking, she pushed the stroller into the man, hoping to knock him down or, at the least, to distract him. She tensed her strong legs and launched herself to the right, drawing her Beretta from the holster at the small of her back.

She cleared leather before her shoulder made contact with the ground. She rolled forward and gained cover behind the closest tree. Its spindly trunk wouldn't provide much, but something was better than nothing.

As soon as Mike saw the man cross the road to intercept Kat, he yelled for the rest of the team. "Get on your feet. Kat needs our help." He snatched up his cell phone and hit the speed dial for the sheriff's office. He crossed the living room and launched himself down the stairwell taking the steps two at a time.

"Eagles Peak Sh…"

Mike cut her off. "FBI, agent Mike Cavanaugh in need of assistance at 643 Dakota Avenue. Sheriff Olsen is aware of this operation. Minimum three car support required. I'm keeping this line open," he said before stuffing the phone into his pocket. He heard the sounds of his team close on his heels.

He reached the bottom of the stairs and arrested his forward progress. He paused for a beat then casually opened the front door and strode out onto the front porch. He heard Jim and Gabe pounding down the stairs behind him. Seeing Mike standing outside of the still open door they held up, waiting for his signal. Mike gave a small nod of his head and then moved down the three steps, turned, and cut to the right, using the Escalade parked in the driveway for cover.

He dropped down on his stomach and used the back tire of the big SUV to hide behind. Two houses over, the man was standing on the sidewalk with a pistol concealed along his leg. He was scanning the road for threats, rapidly looking both up and down the street for anything that looked like trouble. He was also prepared to give cover fire for his friend across the road.

On the other side of the road, Kat was trying to hide behind a spindly tree. It was at best six inches thick. Luckily, she wasn't much thicker, standing sideways behind it. Mike could see the man start to stand up, the doll hanging limply from his beefy hand.

"What the fuck is this?" he asked as he raised his eyes from the doll. He saw her hiding behind the tree. "I think it's time for you to come out so we can talk about this," he said as he brought his gun up and pointed it at Kat.

"Listen, I'm a cop. Put down your gun and lay on the ground. You haven't done anything wrong yet. Don't make this a bad day."

"Ma'am, I'm sorry to tell you but it's already a bad day, and it's about to get a whole lot worse for you. Why don't you just step on out from behind that sorry excuse for a tree before you get hurt? If you look to your left, you'll see my friend already has the drop on you. You have my word as a gentleman that you won't get hurt."

Kat knew she needed to keep him talking. The longer he went on, the more time Mike and the guys had to back her up.

"How do I know that you won't shoot me as soon as I do?"

"Like I said, I'm a gentleman," he said with a smirk. "I don't like to hurt women." He paused before he continued, "I don't like to, but if you don't do what I say and come over here, I will hurt you, now move," he finished with an edge to his voice that wasn't there before. He was dropping the cultured façade and was returning to the true character of what he was, an animal that had his prey cornered.

From this distance, Mike couldn't make out the words Kat was saying, but he could hear enough to know that she was trying the talk the man down. Jim and Gabe had formed up on him at the Escalade.

"What do you want to do Mike?" asked Gabe,

"Go around the back of the house and come up on the other side of this one." He said, indicating the guard that was closest to them.

Mike gave instructions to Jim and then stood up. He made a show of unlocking the Escalade. He acted like he was rummaging around in the back seat, looking for something. He crawled inside the big SUV and made a show of digging around in the back seat for a few seconds before closing the door and walking around to the other side. On his way, he looked up at the man standing on the sidewalk. "Hey, good morning."

The man nodded a greeting to him.

Mike could see that the man across the street was also watching him. "So, are you new here? I don't think I've seen you before."

Fault Line©

Mike could tell that he was frustrating the man. He wanted to watch what was taking place across the street and didn't appreciate the distraction.

"I'm visiting my cousin."

"Hey, that's cool," said Mike. "I know quite a few of the people here. Where does he live?"

"The white one down there," the man said gesturing vaguely down the street.

Mike saw the gun the man was holding along his right leg. He wanted to keep him talking long enough for Gabe to get into position.

"What do you think's going on over there?" Mike asked looking across the road.

"I was wondering the same thing. Looks like a lover's spat to me."

Mike was now standing on the sidewalk, about three feet from the man. They were both facing the street watching the drama unfold.

The man across the road raised his gun and started to turn it towards them.

A Novel by T. L. Scott

Gabe took advantage of the distraction Mike had caused and came out from the side of the house. He was halfway across the lawn when he was punched in the shoulder. The force of the impact spun him around. Disoriented, he found himself lying on the dry grass looking up at the sky. He rolled over onto his stomach and brought his gun up. He tried to bring his left hand up to steady it. The pain from his shoulder was so intense it blurred his vision. An overwhelming ache radiated from his gut throughout the rest of his body. He blinked his eyes to clear his vision and used the ground to support the butt of the gun, elevating the barrel he lined his sights up on where the shot had come from. Not seeing any further threat, he checked his perimeter. Mike had taken the guy down to the ground, and they were battling hand to hand. Gabe quickly shifted his vision across the street. The man was lying on his back, and Kat was cautiously moving toward him. She had her gun trained on him as she approached his inert form.

Fault Line©

Gabe brought his focus back to the two men battling each other fifteen feet from him. Mike was sitting on the guy's chest and was drawing his fist back for the knock-out blow when chunks of dirt started to shoot up into the air to his left.

Gabe rolled to his right. Intense pain radiated throughout his body, each rotation slammed his injured shoulder into the ground. It was so intense it took his breath away. Pain was okay. It meant he was still alive. That sniper could re-engage at any time, and he had no desire to be lying in the open when he decided he wanted to have some more fun.

Seeing the dirt jump into the air around Gabe, Mike knew that a shooter was targeting him. Mike rolled off the guy he had just knocked out. He continued to roll. A stationary target was much easier to hit. He had no intention of making the sniper's job easy. He rolled off the grass and out into the road. The sound of squealing tires caused him to jerk his head around. He was staring at the front end of a car. His view of the vehicle shrank down the closer it came to him. The squad car skidded to a stop; a mere three feet from his head. As soon as it came to a halt, the driver's side door opened, and Sheriff Olsen took cover behind it.

"What's the situation?" he shouted to Mike.

Mike didn't have a chance to answer. Bullets chewed a line across the hood of the car. He shot his gaze up to the second story window of the house next door and saw a muzzle flash as it spat out automatic fire. Mike pivoted on his butt, sitting up and bracing his back against the squad car. He brought his gun up, and aligned his sights with his eye in one fluid, well-practiced motion and squeezed off two bursts of three shots in rapid succession.

When no shots were immediately returned; he moved around the squad car to put the engine block between himself and the shooter. As he came around the front of the car he had his gun trained on the inert form of the man lying on the sidewalk. Kat was kneeling next to him. It looked like she was checking for a pulse with one hand. She had her weapon in the other hand and was training it in a grid, looking for targets.

Mike looked up at the second story window. He didn't know if the shooter was down or just biding his time.

He got his answer as another flash of automatic fire came from the shadows of the window.

Mike immediately returned fire, squeezing off seven more well-placed shots.

"Gabe, you okay?" Mike called out.

"Hit in the shoulder but still in the fight," Gabe answered. "Our guy ran off. He went around the other side of the house. Mike, the sheriff is down."

Mike opened the passenger door of the squad car and keyed the mic on the radio. "Dispatch this is FBI Agent Michael Cavanaugh at 643 Dakota Avenue. Sheriff Olsen is down. What's the status of the back-up I requested?"

"Repeat that Agent; what's your name? Sheriff Olsen is down? How bad's he hurt? Do you need an ambulance? Is he-"

Mike cut her off. "Shots have been fired, and I need those backup units. Calm down and tell me how far out they are."

"Two units are on their way and should be there any time now."

"Agent Cavanaugh," said a calm voice from the back of the patrol car.

Mike whipped his head around. He recognized the man in the back seat as the soldier from last night at *The Thorny Cactus*. Sitting next to him was the same woman who'd been with him. Without giving it another thought, he hit the lock release and went around to open the door.

Mike looked across the street and saw Kat had taken up position behind the tree again. This time she was in a prone position. She was covering his perimeter. He signaled for her to continue watching the area to the south. He looked back at Gabe and directed him to guard the approach to the north. He then dug his phone out of his pocket. "You still there, dispatch?"

"Still here, Agent Cavanaugh," said a different voice than the one he had spoken with before. This woman sounded calm and efficient.

"How close are the units I requested?"

"They should be arriving any second now."

"Direct one to go to the back of 826 Dakota Avenue, using the alley. The other two units need to block off the ends of Dakota Avenue and set up a perimeter. With the shots that have already been fired, I'm surprised we aren't already compromised. This trap is ready to spring, and the cockroaches are going to scramble. If I lose even one of these scumbags, I'm going to be very upset. Do you copy all of that dispatch?"

"Consider it done Agent Cavanaugh. I have additional support on the way. A SART team is responding and will be on site within 15 minutes. Is there any additional support you require?"

"Who am I speaking with?" Mike asked.

"Officer Margaret Rodriguez, sir."

"Officer Rodriguez, we have one casualty and one agent wounded. One aggressor likely a casualty and the status of another is unknown. One aggressor eluded us. We have to move on the target house. Instruct the units that block off the street to contain all personnel. Absolutely no exceptions. I don't care if it's a grandma with her walker! No exceptions!"

"Copy that."

Mike put the phone back into his pocket and turned his attention to Bill and Isabella.

"Ma'am you need to stay in the car."

"No sir, I'm staying with Bill."

"I'm sorry to say that this isn't over yet. Bill, is it?"

Bill gave a small shake of his head as he scanned his eyes down the street.

"Where did you get your training?" Mike asked him.

"Sergeant Bill Thompson." He reached out and shook hands with Mike.

Fault Line©

No mention of your unit? SPECOPS for sure, thought Mike.

"I need your help, Sergeant." Mike filled him in on what he needed him to do and what their objective was. After she had listened to the men discuss the situation they were in, Isabella reluctantly agreed to stay in the car. She would keep dispatch updated on what she saw as the situation developed.

A Novel by T. L. Scott

Chapter 12

Isabella was sitting between the two men, already talking with Officer Rodriguez. Mike looked across the front seat of the sheriff's car. "Bill, are you ready?"

"Yes, sir," he replied.

Mike got out of the car and started walking down the street. Bill followed close behind him. He wasn't surprised to see Kat cutting across the street to meet up with them.

She quickly fell in step with them. They walked a few strides without anyone saying anything. Kat finally broke the silence. "You didn't really think that I would let you have all of the fun, did you?"

"No, not really," Mike replied.

He was glad to have her along. Now that the patrol cars were in place she wasn't needed as a guard. He was afraid that he would need her experience sooner rather than later.

Fault Line©

He led them at an angle to the right, getting off the street where they were a clear target. He felt very exposed being that out in the open. The house next to their target had a nice hedge of bushes that separated the properties. It also had a couple of decent sized trees on each side of the sidewalk which led up to the front door. He wanted to use them for cover. They could easily hide behind the bushes while the re-enforcements formed up.

The sun was shining, and a light breeze was blowing. Birds were singing in the trees. Mike watched a squirrel scramble across the sidewalk. This looked like it was just another ordinary day. If it weren't for these criminals, it would be. It was Mike's job to clean up this mess so this neighborhood could get back to being normal.

He pulled them up when they were close. Kat and Bill fell in behind him. The shrub provided less cover than he'd hoped. The leaves were anything but lush. They could easily see through the bush to their target. That also meant that they could be seen by their targets. Fortunately, if they stayed still then the patterns of the bush would mask their presence. It wasn't ideal, but Mike would take what he could find.

He looked over at Bill. "I want you to double back and then cross the street to the other side," he said showing with his hands where he wanted Bill to go. "Walk casually until you get in front of the house. You see that red Impala?" He asked pointing to the sedan parked in front of the house.

Bill nodded his head that he did.

"Good, I want you over there and covering down on the front of the house." Mike then turned his attention to Kat. "After Bill gets to the other side of the road you start walking on this side. Once you get to the bushes on the far side of the house," he said, pointing to the well-trimmed five-foot tall hedge which separated the two properties, "cut down the side. I don't know on which side of the house the entrance to the backyard is. I want us all to go in at the same time. If it's not this side, then you can wave us off, and we can fall back and re-position on the other side of the target." He paused as he checked his watch. "Okay, we go in three minutes."

Action at the intersection at the south end of the road caught his attention. Two more squad cars pulled up, and people started to form-up. Mike looked back over his shoulder and saw that the same thing was happening at the north end of the street.

"You guys stay here. I'm going back to coordinate these re-enforcements. No, on second thought, go ahead and get into the same positions we talked about. I'll have them form up on you." Bill and Kat nodded their heads that they understood.

Isabella was already in touch with the patrolmen through the radio in the sheriff's car. She was relaying all the updates to Mike on his radio. When Mike got to the car, he briefed everyone on his plans for taking down both targets. He would use some of the men that had just arrived to sweep the other house. He was confident that the sniper was dead, but he wasn't taking any chances.

He also wanted to secure the security house. There might be some intel in there that these guys had left behind.

With his plan communicated, Mike left to lead his strike team. Isabella stayed in the sheriff's car and kept him updated from her position.

The teams were formed up as Mike had directed. In addition, there was a team covering the rear of the house. They had found Jim covering the back of the house, and he had a surprise for them. He had caught the guy that ran off from Mike. He'd positioned himself in a small space between a garage and some shrubs on the far side of the alley. He saw a man come out from behind a house and start to run towards him. The guy stopped and looked both ways before putting his hands on the top of the fence. Jim didn't recognize who the man was, but he knew that if he made it over the fence the whole operation was blown. Jim was up and running before the thought had finished forming in his mind. He had enough room to get a good head of steam. The guy was so focused on what he saw on the other side of the fence that he paused at the top. He never noticed Jim barreling down on him.

It was no contest. Jim wrapped his thickly muscled arms around the guy, tackling him with all 230 pounds of solid muscle, impacting his relaxed form at close to twenty miles an hour. The force of the impact carried the men six feet through the air until they hit the dry, hard ground. Jim kept the man under him so his target took the brunt of the impact. By the time Jim had drug him to the end of the block and put the insta-cuffs on him, the guy was finally coming back around.

Having turned his charge over to a uniformed officer to hold in the van, he was able to focus on the take-down of the house. He was now in charge of the team that would make their assault over the fence. They had found several places where they could look through the fence and see what was happening in the backyard. They were set and ready to go when the time came to execute the take-down.

The four different teams were now talking with each other thanks to the hand-held radios the re-enforcements had brought with them. The majority of this rag-tag force were regular patrolmen, and this type of operation was not what they were used to doing. They weren't used to it, but they had all been trained and were ready to execute their assigned tasks.

Bill stepped out from behind the red Impala he'd been using for cover. He made a show of looking at a piece of paper in his hand and then looking up at the houses along the street. He looked up and down from the paper to the houses. He was working at making it obvious he was comparing what was written on the paper with the address of the house as he approached it.

"He's approaching the steps," squawked out from the radio. Mike listened to the progress as it was relayed to him over the radio.

"He's looking at the paper again. Okay, he just rang the doorbell."

Fault Line©

"I have movement in the window to the left of the door. Male, late twenties to early thirties, answered the door." As soon as the door was opened loud music flooded out of the house.

"Hi, I think I'm in the right place," said Bill. "My wife told me to pick up our daughter at a birthday party, and this is the address she gave me. I really hope this is the right place," he said, raising his voice to be heard over the music.

The man opened the door a little wider and looked around outside. Seeing nothing out of place, he brought his attention back to Bill. "What's your daughter's name?"

"What," he asked, cupping his hand to his ear.

"What's your daughter's name?" the man asked again.

Bill smiled at the man. "Her name is Amy. I'm sure she's having an exciting time, and I don't want to take her away before she's ready."

The man must have liked what he heard. "Come on in," he said as he stepped to the side to let Bill pass. "The girls are in the backyard playing."

"Hold positions. We have a friendly inside. Bad guy is still looking around. A couple of ticks went by. Okay, the door's closed, I don't see any more movement at the window. Your call Red Lead," reported the spotter that was posted across the street from the house.

"On my mark red, yellow, blue teams execute. Green, five seconds then execute, Mark," Mike called out.

He held up his hand and ticked off three seconds before sprinting for the side of the house and the small space that led to the gate into the backyard. It was only four feet wide, and half-way down most of that space was taken up by a central air unit.

Mike checked his speed and pivoted around the unit. He cautiously moved closer to the gate. Once his team had formed up behind him, he reached out his hand and unlatched the gate in the fence then casually strolled into the backyard as if he belonged there. He nodded his head and gave a half-hearted smile at the people closest to him. His eyes quickly darted around the decent sized yard quickly assessing the scene. There were about fifteen girls ranging in age from four to ten or eleven playing together. Their party dresses and hair bouncing as they ran around chasing each other. It really looked like a birthday party. There was even a table with cake and snacks loaded upon it. A bouncy castle that was actually in the shape of a castle was blown up off to the side with four or five girls playing inside. Mike saw that there were nine men and three women mostly gathered close to the food who were looking increasingly nervous. Two men were stationed close to the gate he had just come through, and another pair of men were positioned close to the back fence-line.

The guards closest to Mike stepped up to him and his entourage. The lead guy, slimmer than his partner by at least a hundred pounds and shorter by nearly a foot started talking.

"Sir, officers, this is a private party. We didn't call for any assistance. What's going on?" he asked in a warm voice. He had his hands spread away from his body with the palms facing Mike. A classic pose to show he meant no harm. His whole demeanor was meant to be disarming and project that there was no reason for them to linger.

"Well, that is good news. Isn't it officers?" Mike asked his men as they were spreading out from behind him, positioning themselves at better angles in case this escalated.

Addressing the smaller of the two men again he said, "we didn't receive a call from this residence for assistance. I'm glad we didn't get our orders wrong," he said, flashing a disarming smile of his own. He looked around at his men. Confident they were in position, he brought his smile and focus back to the two men in front of him.

"We got a call that a missing girl was identified as being on these premises. Do you know anything about that?" he asked with a smile. Mike was looking at the smaller of the two men but could see the bigger man getting agitated. His big shoulders were tensing for action. Unlike his diminutive friend, his hands were not on display. They were hidden behind his back. Mike had also tracked in his peripheral vision that the other two men along the back fence-line had separated and were lining up to catch them in a crossfire. They didn't have time to react to this change before men came pouring over the back fence-line.

Mike reacted immediately and shot his hand out, grabbing the small man by the wrist and pulling him into his body. He wrapped his other arm around the man's neck. He used the momentum to spin them around. Pivoting on his right foot, he brought his left leg up to deliver a nasty kick to the big man's head. The force of the unexpected blow toppled the man to the ground. As he fell, he lost his grip on the gun he'd been hiding behind his back. Mike continued the movement, rolling to his right and coming up on his right knee with his left foot planted on the other side of the smaller man. Two of the men in uniform had landed on top of the bigger man and were putting insta-cuffs on his wrists and feet.

"Everybody just stay nice and calm. The party's over," Mike announced in his practiced calm authoritarian voice. He looked around for any threats that hadn't been neutralized yet.

A man on the far side of the yard, closer to the bouncy castle, began to reach behind his back when he was hit from behind and thrown to the ground.

Yellow team had just come through the bushes that lined that side of the property. "Now would be a good time for all of you to lie down for a bit," he said to the adults who had not already been forced to do so.

"Kids, why don't you all go over to the sand box and . . "

The sharp crack of shots fired inside the house punctured the air over the deep base thumping of the music.

Mike jumped up and sprinted toward the house.

Fault Line©

Kat reached the back door just before him. "Getting slow in your old age, boss."

She threw open the screen door and went in low. Mike went in high. They cleared the back porch like they'd done on countless other raids. The source of the music was a stereo with two tower speakers pushing out kids singing along to some modern music. Kat punched the power button, silencing the tunes.

The wooden door into the house was standing open, so they continued with their momentum. They found themselves in a sparsely decorated kitchen. The central feature was an island in the middle of the room. A quick glance to his right and Mike was looking at the dining room. Uniformed officers were moving in the reflection from the china cabinet. "Red team in the kitchen area."

"Blue team here, all clear."

"What's the sitrep?" asked Mike.

"We encountered resistance from two hostiles in the living room. They're out of action. We're clearing the upstairs now."

When Bill got inside, he saw there was another man in the living room. He was sitting on a couch on the left side of the room. He had his gun out on display. Bill quickly looked away. He didn't want the man to think he was challenging him.

"Come on," said the man that had opened the door. Bill followed him towards the dining room.

The loud sound of the front door being broken down drove Bill into action. He lashed out and punched the man in front of him in the kidney then wrapped his left arm around the man's throat. He wrenched his neck to turn the man, using his body for cover. The man from the couch stood up and managed to get off a couple shots at the men pouring into the front of the house before he was taken down hard by three shots to his chest.

Fault Line©

The man Bill had by the throat took advantage of the distraction and slammed his head back into Bill's face. Stunned, Bill loosened his grip a fraction, just enough for the man to break free from his hold. The man lurched away from him. He didn't make it any further before he was taken out by one of the uniformed officers.

Bill's eyes watered from the blow to his nose making his vision distorted. He didn't think it was broken, but if so, he'd deal with it when this was over. He signaled for his team to form up on him. He blinked his eyes rapidly to clear them. Satisfied that he was back in the fight, he paused at the foot of the stairs. He took a breath and made eye contact with the men lined up to follow him. Satisfied with what he saw, he gave a small nod of his head.

He took a quick look around the corner. All clear! He took the stairs two at a time, rushing to clear the top floor of any aggressors.

Bill was at the end of the upstairs hallway with two uniformed men of the blue team. They'd already cleared two bedrooms. The only room left was this last one that faced the front of the house. They hadn't met any resistance since they made their initial entry and had cleared the living room. His head was still throbbing, but at least his eyes had stopped watering.

He took hold of the bronze, latch style, door handle in his hand. Looking over his shoulder he mouthed a countdown from three, two, one, then pushed down on the handle. Locked. He was barely able to stop his momentum before he slammed into the still closed door. He didn't want to make a lot of noise by breaking down the door, but they had to get in there.

He directed the men with him to push on the door together hoping that their combined efforts would overpower the frame. His plan worked surprisingly well, and the door flew open without making a lot of noise.

The men came through fast, scrambling to train their weapons around the space. Bill continued across the pink carpet to the far side of the room. A queen size bed took up the center of the room. A dresser with a TV on it sat across from the bed. A large window with a cushion on the overlarge sill looked out on the front of the house. A door on the left of the bed was closed. The men quickly confirmed that the room was empty of threats. As Bill had expected, this door was also locked.

"You need to come out of there. Open the door nice and slow and keep your hands where I can see them." Bill and the men stood off to the side of the door, ready for what might come through it.

"This is your last warning before we come in." He was surprised to see the knob turn. The door slowly opened about a foot. The men's attention was tightly focused on what was on the other side. When nothing more happened for a couple of beats, Bill addressed the person again. "Listen, we're the police, we're not going to hurt you. Come on out so we can help you," he said.

"You come in," said the voice of a little girl.

Bill had seen too much to think that the situation was all clear just because a little girl had talked to him. He had no idea what he would be facing on the other side of that door except that there was a scared little girl in there. That didn't mean that there wasn't someone else there as well.

He hooked his foot around the door, nudging it open, he came through the door frame. He found himself in a closet with clothes neatly hanging on both sides. Women's clothes were on the left, and men's lined the right. At the other end of the closet, a door was open leading into a bathroom. He had a clear view of the right side of the room. He could see a porcelain sink and a toilet. The light from the ceiling and the two lights above the sink made the white tiles on the floor stand out. He stepped to his left, leaning his body into dresses on their hangers, trying to get a better look. He used the mirror over the sink to see what was hidden behind the door. He could make out a little girl sitting in the bathtub. The shower curtain was only partially open. It obstructed his view of the rest of the tub.

"Okay, I'm here. Are you alone sweetie?" Bill asked as he raked his hands through the hanging clothes to ensure what he already knew. He was alone in the closet.

"Yes, it's just me. You're not a bad man are you."

"No sweetie, I'm one of the good guys. I'm here to help you. Why don't you come out of the bathtub nice and slow? I don't want you to fall down trying to climb out." Bill could see the shower curtain begin to move and a little black-haired girl of about eight climbed out of the tub.

"You're a very brave girl. Stay right there for a second; I'm coming in. Everything's going to be okay." Bill kept talking with her in a reassuring tone while he entered the small space. He swept the curtain back on the tub to confirm it was empty. The girl was alone. Seeing no threats, he sat down on the edge of the bathtub and looked directly at her for the first time. She had light blue eyes set in her round face. He realized that this little girl was the same one he'd seen the other day looking out of her window.

"Are you okay sweetie?" Bill asked her.

She nodded her head.

"Okay, look through the closet. Do you see those police officers? You know the police are your friends. They're here to help you, okay?"

The girl looked up at him with a blank look on her pretty little face.

"Everything's going to be okay sweetie." He reached out and took her hand in his. "What's your name, honey?"

"Isabella," she said.

"Well, Isabella, my name's Bill. What do you say we get out of here?"

"I'm not supposed to leave the room. Miguel says it's not safe. I can only leave if he's with me."

"Is Miguel here?"

"No," she said. "He was earlier. He said he'd be back."

"Is Miguel your brother?"

"No, I don't have any family. My Mommy was taken away."

Fault Line©

"I'm sorry honey. Who's Miguel?"

"He was mommies friend."

"Listen, I know another Isabella that would be very happy to meet you. In fact, she has pretty hair just like you. Would you like to meet her?"

The little girl nodded her head.

"Okay, let's get out of here," said Bill.

They went back out through the closet with her little hand holding his strong callused one. Once they were in her room, they stopped so she could look around at the familiar space. The police officers moved out of the room. Bill was following the last man out when he felt Isabella stop short of the door. He turned back to her.

"What is it, honey?"

"I can't leave my room without permission. Miguel would be really mad."

Bill lowered himself to a knee. "He's not going to hurt you any more honey, you're. . ."

The little girl shook her head sharply from side to side.

"Really, Isabella, I promise you Miguel isn't going to hurt you. You're safe now."

"No, Miguel doesn't hurt me. He used to hurt mommy, but he never hurt me. But if I leave my room, he'll be real mad. I don't want him to yell at me. He scares me when he's mad."

"I understand, sweetie; today is different though. The police are here to try and figure out what's been happening. Do you think you can help us to understand what Miguel and his friends have been doing? "

"I don't think so."

"That's okay, sweetie. We just want to talk and try to understand. Is that okay?" Bill asked her.

She nodded her head and scrunched up her face as only a child can do.

"What do you say we go downstairs?"

Isabella reached out and retook his hand.

Fault Line©

Chapter 13

Mike was walking to the living room from the kitchen when he noticed a door on his left. It was a white panel door with a simple brass door knob like all of the other doors in the house. The only difference with this one was the heavy-duty stainless-steel lock hasp. The lock was not in it, and when he tested the door, he found the knob unlocked as well.

"Do these places usually have a basement?" he asked the officer in uniform standing behind him.

"No, they don't," he responded.

"Want to go see what one looks like?" Mike asked. Without waiting for an answer, he opened the door and led the four officers, who made up his team, into the space below. A dim bulb was already lit. Its pale light illuminated a carpeted staircase leading down ten steps into the finished basement.

A Novel by T. L. Scott

Mike held his position at the top of the stairs, straining his ears, listening for any sound of danger. The muffled sound of music was all he heard. It was probably coming from behind a closed door, he thought.

Not seeing any shadows moving, he cautiously made his way down the wooden stairs one step at a time. At the bottom, the stairwell opened onto a hallway with three doors painted in different bright colors on each side. Mike signaled with his hands for each man to take a door for a coordinated sweep. That left one door at the end of the hall uncovered. He wasn't a superstitious man, but the fact it was a red door gave him pause. He didn't like leaving any possible area as an open threat while they cleared the other rooms. It was a risk he had to accept though.

He signaled the men to get ready for the assault. He held up his right hand in a closed fist. His left hand firmly grasped the door handle of the yellow door. He dropped his right hand signaling his team to execute their search while his left hand threw open the door into the yellow room.

It turned out that Mike made the right call. There hadn't been a reason to worry about the last door. It was the utility room containing the furnace and hot water heater. Red made sense now knowing what was inside that room.

Behind the other doors, they found rooms decorated to look like an ordinary little girl's room, with pink wallpaper, frilly curtains, stuffed animals, and a queen size bed which took up most of the available space. There were also video cameras set on tripods to record the sick perversions that the team interrupted. Six men were caught in various stages of offenses, actively perpetrating their crimes on their innocent victims. Eight little girls, ranging in age from six to eleven, were rescued.

The men were placed under arrest and escorted, none too gently, out of the basement. From the opinion of the arresting officers, it was a little satisfying that two of the men resisted their arrest. It just so happened that they needed to have their resistance broken before they were carried out to the waiting vehicle. Medical assistance was rendered to the men once they were strapped to the gurney. None of their injuries were life-threatening, but they would be cared for as if they were. These men would be fit for their trial and held accountable for their actions.

The girls were kept in the basement hallway until officers from the Special Victims Unit could arrive to process them. They would need special care. It would start with medical care to attend to their physical injuries. Paramedics were already there, screening the girls for any external injuries. They appeared to be in pretty good health. They were well nourished and hydrated. One of the little girls had suffered some contusions at the hands of her abuser. She was getting them tended to in one of the rooms. Physically they looked like they would be okay.

Fault Line©

Once they were processed in, other doctors would help to treat the emotional abuse they had suffered. Efforts would be made to locate these girls' families. The care these girls would get would last for years to come. Mike knew that even the most optimistic outcome would be that these children would be dealing with the injuries they suffered, at the hands of these sick criminals, for the rest of their lives. It was the job of Mike and the rest of the people in law enforcement to see to it that these men suffered at least as long.

Bill kept the little girl, Isabella, with him. He resisted surrendering her to the SVU arguing that she had been found upstairs and not in the basement. It was thin, he knew, but he also knew that there was something about this little girl that separated her from the rest of the little girls that had been victimized here. If Mike's partner Kat hadn't intervened, he would have lost that battle.

"Hey Isabella, do you see that woman that just walked in? The one with the pretty black hair?" Bill asked her as he pointed to Isabella.

She paused just inside of the door and, seeing Bill pointing at her, she pointed at herself and mouthed "Me?"

Bill obliged by smiling and nodding his head in an exaggerated fashion. Turning to little Isabella he said in a voice like a whisper "See, I told you she was pretty."

"She is," agreed the little girl.

"Am I interrupting?" Isabella asked as she knelt down in front of the little girl. She couldn't help noticing the familiarity of her features. She looked so much like her little sister it was disconcerting. The only difference was the piercing blue of the girl's eyes. It was too much to hope that she had at long last found a link to Sara. She had followed her disappointing trail for long enough to know that all too many little girls, and grown women, bore a striking resemblance to her sister.

Fault Line©

"What's your name sweetie?" Isabella asked her. She didn't fail to notice the small look the girl gave to Bill and the corresponding nod he replied with.

"I'm Isabella, same as you."

"No sweetie, I don't think so," replied Isabella.

Confused, little Isabella looked at Bill.

"You're not the same as me, honey. You are much prettier," said Isabella with a big smile. "How old are you honey?"

"Eight," little Isabella replied.

"Are you sure? I thought you were at least 10. You're a big girl for your age."

"I'm kind of short for my age," replied the little girl in a meek voice.

Isabella reached out and gently raised the little girl's face with a gentle touch of her finger under her chin. "How tall you are is not the only way you are measured. I can see that you are strong beyond your years, Isabella. I am very happy to meet you."

172

Bill saw the tentative smile that flitted across the little girl's mouth.

Isabella reached out, and the little girl took her hand. "You can call me, Izzy," she told Isabella.

"I like it. I thought you looked like an Izzy," Isabella said with a big smile. She looked over at Bill and asked, "what do we do now?"

He was saved from telling her that he didn't know when Mike came into the living room.

He strode over to them and squatted down in front of little Izzy, bringing his six-foot-two frame more or less to her eye level. "Are you feeling good enough to talk with me a little bit?" he asked her. "My name's Mike, and I'm with the FBI. I need you to answer a couple of questions for me."

"Am I under arrest?" asked the little girl. She squeezed Isabella's hand and looked to Bill for reassurance.

Mike smiled at her. "No sweetie. You aren't in any trouble. We're just trying to figure out what was going on here. What you tell us will help us to figure things out. No one is going to hurt you. I promise you that things are going to be okay now. All of these police officers are here to help you and your friends," he said sweeping his arm around.

She looked around at all the people moving around the house. "They're not my friends," Izzy said, looking down at her tennis shoes. They had bright colored flowers on them, and they lit up with a pink light as she shuffled her feet back and forth.

"What do you mean they're not your friends, honey?" asked Isabella.

"He never lets me play with them," Izzy said.

Mike noticed that the little girl visibly relaxed as she shifted her attention to the woman.

"He always says I have to stay in my room where it's safe."

"Safe from what?" asked Mike.

"The bad people that are looking for me. He said if they find me, they'll take me away like they took away my mom."

"How long has she been gone, sweetie?"

"I was six when they took her away." Her gaze had returned back to her shoes. They were no longer lighting up. Her feet hung listlessly, a few inches from the floor.

"What do you mean they took her?" asked Mike. "Did you see somebody take her?"

She shook her head. Her face was hidden under her black hair. "No, but he said that if I wasn't careful, and behaved, they'd come and take me away too," she mumbled.

"Izzy," said Mike.

Her gaze remained focused on her shoes.

Isabella rubbed her hand on the little girls back as she held her little hand with the other one.

After a couple of seconds without a response from the little girl Mike continued, "No one is going to take you away. You're safe now." The little girl still didn't raise her eyes.

"Izzy, Bill isn't going to let anyone hurt you."

She looked up at Bill and saw that he was shaking his head.

"Nope, nobody is going to hurt you or take you away. You're safe now."

Izzy looked at Isabella next.

"It's true sweetie. You're safe."

"Izzy, do you see all the people here? They are all police officers, and they are all here to make sure you're safe," said Mike.

She watched all the people walking throughout the house for a minute. Without saying another word, she leaned into the gentle embrace of the woman that was holding onto her.

Mike and Bill exchanged a look. They both knew she needed some quiet comforting. They stood up and moved towards the kitchen so they could talk.

Mike's cell phone started to vibrate. He pulled it out and read the message on the screen: *Lots of activity. In position.*

He sent off a quick response: B thr n ten. Ur call b4

"What's your cell number?" he asked Bill.

As soon as Mike finished entering it into his phone, it rang. He answered it and then almost immediately hung it up.

"Call me if you need to. I have to go. This isn't over yet."

He shook hands with Bill. "Thank you for your help Sergeant."

Mike rushed out the front door and bumped into Deputy Gonzales. The two men bounced off each other and barely avoided falling off the small porch.

"Are you okay?" asked Mike as he pin-wheeled his arms to avoid falling into the bushes that fronted the house.

Fault Line©

Gonzales's hand shot out and grabbed the front of the blazer with FBI emblazoned on it, pulling enough for Mike to catch his balance. "Yeah, you?" he asked.

"Good, thanks." And with that Mike was off at a sprint.

Bill was walking back to sit down next to the girls again when he saw Lieutenant Gonzales come in through the front door. "I'll be right back," he said to Isabella. He made sure she saw him look over at Gonzales before he walked away.

They met at the entrance to the living room.

Gonzales kept his voice low. "So, were you able to find out anything more about what was going on here Bill?"

"Not really. One thing is strange, though. For some reason, they kept that little girl separate from the rest. I don't know for sure, but it doesn't sound like she was abused like the rest of the girls."

"That's good news, at least for her. It is strange though. Anything else?" Gonzales said.

"The little girl, her name is Isabella, said that a man named Miguel was the one that kept her in her room. Sounds like he was in charge here. She also said that bad men came and took her mom away two years ago. She's been with this Miguel for at least that long."

Gonzales didn't say anything. Bill could tell he was trying to fit this latest information into the story he was trying to piece together.

Gonzales turned his head and looked at Bill. He opened his mouth as if he was about to say something and then looked as if he thought better of it and closed it again. He gave his head a small shake as if trying to dislodge a piece of the puzzle that didn't fit.

Bill saw Gonzales turn his head and take in the activity that was still going on around them. After a minute he focused his eyes back on Bill. "The girls are being taken to the hospital to be processed. The van left with them a few minutes ago."

"I'll give you a ride back to the ranch," he said, looking over at the girls sitting on the couch. Isabella was braiding Izzy's hair. "That woman is staying at the Lookout Lodge, right? I can see the little girl is attached to her."

Gonzales thought it over for a minute. "She can ride with me while I bring the girl to the hospital. We'll go there after I drop you off at the ranch," he said as he shifted past Bill and walked across the living room to the couch. He stopped suddenly and turned back to Bill, who had been following a half step behind him. Bill pulled up short to avoid bumping into him.

"When I was coming into the house I bumped into Agent Cavanaugh. Where was he off to in such a hurry?"

"I don't know Jorge, he got a text and then left, he didn't say where he was going."

Lieutenant Gonzales nodded his head. "I would have thought he would have stayed here until the scene was processed," he said to himself as he continued on his way to the ladies sitting on the couch.

A Novel by T. L. Scott

Chapter 14

The ominous clouds had been piling up throughout the afternoon. Shortly after nightfall, they opened up, releasing their pent-up load on the dry, cracked hardpan. Visibility was quickly reduced to less than thirty feet. The sheets of rain came down at a sharp angle, pushed by the high winds. The weather, as nasty as it was, worked to the advantage of the patchwork team Mike had assembled. Kat had coordinated the initial assault with the first units on the scene. They were prepared to eliminate the perimeter sentries before the main attack on the warehouse.

In the forty-five minutes since they had been in place, the action around the warehouse had slowed. Kat briefed Mike, upon his arrival on the scene, that two tractor trailers, one cargo van, and a horse carrier had already departed from the warehouse. The vehicles had left separately. They couldn't tell what, if anything, was inside them from their positions. She had contacted the State Police, and they had issued a BOLO on the vehicles. Mike was confident that they'd be caught in the net that was quickly constricting.

He wasn't surprised to discover that Kat had deployed their hodge-podge assault team just as he would have done. A team was in place on each side of the warehouse to cover the assault on the flanks and, if needed, to provide lateral support and suppression fire. The two primary attack points were the big vehicle doors at each end of the warehouse. Unfortunately, the big doors were closed, blocking them from seeing what was going on inside. Mike still had a couple of tricks up his sleeve. What he didn't have, he knew, was time.

He knew their best move was to go in fast and use surprise to their advantage. The storm was masking them from view, and the howling winds and thunder covered the minimal sounds they made. It also would cost them sure footing. For the teams that would be providing cover from up here, it was not an issue. For the two assault teams, it was a different story. The earth had been baked so dry over the summer that it wasn't absorbing the water pouring down on it. Small rivers ran down the hill to the gravel that surrounded the warehouse. Where there wasn't water flowing, the hard ground had a layer of mud mixed with clay that made everything slippery. It was not the ideal situation, but, in his experience, it never was.

"Kat, I wish we could assault the front door head-on. But I don't see a way we can get down there without being lit up by those lights," he said pointing to the front of the warehouse where two streetlights lit up the area. The arcs lit up the perimeter to about two hundred feet. It was too much ground to cross without being seen.

"Jim could take them out easily."

"Probably, but once he shot out that first light our element of surprise is blown, and we still have fifty meters to cover. We'd be running headlong into what could be a full defensive wall. If we take that tack, we would still need to get around, or through, the warehouse to secure the back door. What we would gain by better footing we would lose a lot more tactically."

"Yeah, I know you're right. I just don't want to fall on my ass, break an ankle, and not be there to back your old ass up."

"It's a risk we'll have to take." Mike knew that Kat was light on her feet and wasn't worried about her falling down. He was worried about *him* breaking something. He went through a mental check as he assessed his thrown together team.

"Keep an eye on your team."

Kat rolled her eyes at him. "Come on, boss. This isn't my first dance."

"I know, Kat. This is different though. These guys are regular cops. From the looks of some of them, the most exercise they have had for quite a while has been lifting a doughnut to their lips."

"That was a good one," she replied with a big smile. "Almost time," she said as she checked her watch.

The seconds ticked down closer to "go" time.

A Novel by T. L. Scott

Mike called in his final instructions and set the assault launch. He would lead a team and converge on the front door while Kat led her team to the back. The team on the other side of the warehouse would do the same. They were closing a wedge on both ends and had personnel staying on the ridge to provide cover from on high. They had the cover of dark, reduced visibility, noise from the storm to cover what little sound they would make getting down to the warehouse, and the element of surprise was on their side. What they didn't have was solid intel on what they'd be facing from inside the warehouse. Well, it wasn't the first time.

"Be advised we have headlights approaching," reported the rear-guard Mike had left to watch the access road.

"Assault team hold. What type of vehicle is it?"

"medium sized moving truck, about a thirty-footer, just passed our location."

"Copy," replied Mike. "Assault team, same plan as before except for a minor change." As soon as he was done explaining the change he deployed both teams. The time they had been up on the ridge, he'd been able to study the slope they were now descending. He took what he thought was the best angles and was surprised to find that it wasn't as bad as he had feared. It was still pretty bad. The team came down the ridge in a semi-controlled slide. Mike kept the headlights from the approaching truck in his line of sight. He had to time their approach just right. If they arrived too early, they could be caught out in the open with the headlights illuminating them for anyone to see.

Mike saw that Kat had her team in place at the rear doors and was ready to go. He checked the status of the other two teams by clicking the mike. He received two clicks each from each team just as the truck was coming to a stop in front of the warehouse.

Two sentries were posted at the big garage door. One guy approached the driver while the other one held back, keeping guard. This was a crucial point. He hoped that nobody tried any heroics and took out the sentries too early.

He let out a breath he didn't know he'd been holding. The garage door opened, and the truck started to ease its way forward. They quickly crossed the open ground. Their footfalls on the gravel sounded like explosions to his ears. He knew the storm would mask their noise but knowing that and feeling good about it were not the same thing at the moment.

They formed up on the side of the warehouse and quickly moved to the corner of the building. Mike watched the progress of the truck with a mirror he held low to the ground, angled around the corner. The fat drops of rain splashed up off the gravel and spotted up the mirror. He was able to make out the big shape of the truck. As soon as the front tires passed over the threshold, entering the warehouse, he dropped his left arm, signaling Kat to start the rear assault. Seconds later, fury was unleashed. The sound of gunfire lit up the night.

Mike and his team took advantage of the confusion and entered the fight.

Inside the door, on the right, three men were trying to figure out what was happening at the back of the building. Mike took advantage of the distraction and focused on the truck, knowing his team would take care of the men. He jumped up on the step, threw open the door, and grabbed the startled passenger's shirt with both hands. Without a pause, he launched himself backward, twisting in the air so that he landed on top of the man before he had a chance to realize what was happening to him. The force of landing on the concrete with Mike's additional hundred and ninety-pound frame on top of him increased the force exponentially. His head slammed onto the concrete, rendering him immediately unconscious.

Mike rolled off the inert form and checked where he'd identified the three threats by the door. His men now occupied that area, so he scanned for other threats. He checked high first. He saw the silhouette of a man up in the rafters. His attention was on the melee at the back of the warehouse. Mike took the initiative and dropped him. His body fell sixty feet, bouncing off wooden crates before impacting the unforgiving concrete floor.

The moving truck stopped, effectively blocking the door.

Weapons fire came from deep inside the warehouse. Mike rolled to his right and took cover behind some crates that were stacked three high. From his vantage point, he saw a pair of legs land on the floor on the other side of the truck. It looked like the pants were the same material as the uniform of some of his team members. He wasn't taking any chances. A sound to his right alerted him to movement. He spun and caught himself before drawing down on the rest of his team as they formed up on him.

"Did any of you see what we're up against," Mike asked. He wasn't happy with the information he received. There were between fifteen and thirty men. He'd seen for himself that there were two small buses, a couple of vans, some cars, and a big SUV. The situation wasn't good, but he knew through hard-won experience that staying in one location was the worst thing that he could do.

He knew Kat and the rest of the team were taking care of business at the other end and they had the gang caught in the middle. "Let's move out," he said, knowing the men would follow him.

He went out fast and low to the side of the truck, firing at targets as they presented themselves. Pushing his back up against the truck he turned to the side, presenting as small of a target as possible. He laid down suppression fire to cover the rest of his team. The third man out from the row was hit at least twice and went down. Going against natural instinct, and with years of training he moved out fast. "Move, move, move," he yelled at his men as he ran deeper into the building, toward the muzzle flashes, and into the fight.

The battle was over a couple minutes later. Eleven bad guys were still alive although it didn't look good for two of them. Eighteen bad guys had lost their lives during the battle along with three team members and two girls that had been held captive in cages. The medics were tending to the wounded while the team began to process the scene.

Mike focused on the task of questioning the prisoners while Kat and two female uniformed officers questioned the women. They quickly learned that a group of men was being held in a shipping container at the back of the warehouse. The men had been kept inside that steel box for a long time. They were gaunt and nearly dead from dehydration.

Mike didn't like what he was hearing on the radio. Support was having trouble getting to them. The storm was the edge of the hurricane, and it was wreaking havoc on the area. The main road from town was flooded out. They wouldn't be receiving any additional support or back-up for at least another thirty minutes.

Fault Line©

Chapter 15

The wheels of the squad car thumped along in rhythm with the old concrete slabs of the road. The steady sound, mixed with the gentle rocking of the car, lulled Izzy into a light sleep. She was laying across the seat, her head resting on Isabella's lap. Isabella was running her fingers through the child's long black hair.

The rain was coming down so hard that it splashed back up off the hood, further reducing the already limited visibility. The headlights barely pierced the deluge. Deputy Gonzalez slowed the car to little more than a creep, his vision intently focused on the road ahead.

Bill strained his eyes to see what lay ahead. The upcoming Appaloosa River was known to overflow its banks and make the bridge impassable. He looked out the side window at the drowned landscape they were driving through and wondered if they would be able to make it in time. It wouldn't be the first time that a downpour had made him detour around to the next crossing. He wasn't worried about his parents. The ranch was on higher ground, and they rarely had to deal with flooding on the property. The area around the ranch could become so saturated that it felt like they were on an island.

He looked into the back again and saw Isabella gazing out of the window. Her lovely face was reflected in the darkened glass. He didn't want to intrude on her thoughts, so he didn't say anything. He didn't miss seeing the crease of skin between her eyes. His mother called it a worry line. It gave away the overall blank expression on her face. She was concerned as well.

So much had happened over the past couple of days. She certainly had enough reasons to be concerned. He couldn't help feeling that there was more trouble out there. Here, inside the squad car, he felt a sense of safety. They were traveling in their secure bubble through the tumultuous storm. He knew this feeling could prove to be a very transient thing.

Fault Line©

"Shit," mumbled Gonzales.

He slowed the cruiser to a stop and then began to back-up. They had overshot the entrance to the driveway. Visibility was now so bad that the headlights could only pierce a couple of feet through the curtain of rain. The wind had also picked up so much that the gusts were noticeably buffeting the car.

Bill was grateful his father always made sure the drive was in good shape. He made sure everything was in good shape. Growing up on the ranch he had instilled the same hard work ethic in him. He knew it was one of the reasons he was a good soldier and he appreciated his father for being such a good example for him to follow, especially at times like this when his lessons became so obvious.

The long drive came up to the side of the house and then split. One branch ended at the back of the house, and the other continued to the barn. Deputy Gonzales eased the car to a stop where the two split. Lights were on in the house and in the barn. The warm light was a welcome sight after fighting their way through the dark of the storm.

"I'll walk in with you, Bill," said Deputy Gonzales. "I want to talk with your dad about something." He looked into his rearview mirror. "You ladies okay to sit a spell? I'll only be a minute."

"We'll be fine, sir," replied Isabella. Izzy nodded her head after she saw the smile on the woman's face.

"Alright then, I'll be back in a minute," he told them.

Bill had been looking at the girls throughout the exchange. "If you don't have plans for breakfast I can pick you up at say eight," Bill offered.

"That sounds good," Isabella replied.

Izzy chuckled and tried to hide it behind her hand.

"What's so funny?" Isabella demanded. "A girl's gotta eat you know."

Izzy waved her hand for Isabella to lean over towards her and then whispered in her ear.

"He likes you."

Isabella turned her head and then returned a whisper into the girl's ear. "Just a secret between us girls?" she asked. She felt Izzy nodding her head enthusiastically. "I like him too."

Izzy couldn't contain her giggles.

"What's so funny?" Bill asked.

"Oh, nothing, it's just girl talk. You boys go on ahead. Us girls will be just fine," she said with a smile on her beautiful face.

"Okay, ladies," replied Bill with a big smile.

Deputy Gonzales had been watching the exchange as well. He didn't have a smile on his face. It was set in a blank expression that defied interpretation.

He looked at Bill. "You ready?"

"It was very nice to meet you, Izzy. I'll come by and see you tomorrow too," Bill told the girl.

"Okay," she replied.

Bill nodded at Gonzales and then opened the door to get out.

Deputy Gonzales already had his door open and was getting out when the window in his door exploded. The impact threw him out of the car's door frame.

Bill was a beat slower than Gonzales to get out of the car. Hearing the crack of the gunshot shatter the night, he immediately dropped to the ground and rolled away from the vehicle. He swung his head around to get his bearings. The shot either came from the barn or somewhere in that direction. With that knowledge, he sprang to his feet and ran to take cover behind the squad car.

"Isabella, get down on the floorboard. Stay DOWN!"

"We are. What's going on?" she asked.

Bill dropped down and looked under the car. Gonzalez was lying on his back. His face turned to the side. It looked like he was looking under the car. The illusion was compelling, but his eyes were closed. The rain pelting off his left cheek should have quickly brought him back to his senses. He couldn't see whether his chest was rising and falling and with the light from the house, he couldn't tell whether there was blood gathering in the pools of water he was lying in.

Thankfully there hadn't been any more shots fired. This was good and bad. It meant that the shooter was disciplined. Bill knew that the reason he hadn't been hit was because the shooter had been focused on the most likely target. There had to be a driver of the vehicle. This meant that the shooter was probably not able to see well either. This was a good thing. It meant he likely didn't have thermal imaging. The light from the house and the flood lamps lit up the drive and made night vision useless.

Bill knew his choices were limited. In fact, there were only three that he could see. One, He could stay there, behind the car, and wait for the shooter to come to him. Definitely not a good option. The shooter could flank him on the right and take him out or come around the far side of the house on his left, and he was equally dead. Option two, the most likely option and the one with the most probability of survival, he could run to his right, away from the lights, and try to circle around on the shooter. The problem was that the shooter would see what he was doing and be watching for him to come out of the shadows. Not good odds at all. Then there was option three, go to the left, to the house. He would be lit up like a Christmas tree by the flood lights and the light coming from the windows of the house. On the plus side though, the distance from the car to the side of the house was only about fifteen feet, four steps. He would only be exposed for about a second. With the reduced visibility and knowing that the shooter had to keep checking his sights on both sides of the car, Bill knew what he had to do.

He shot out from behind the car. On the second step, his foot slipped in the muck, and he fell to the left, his feet scrambling for purchase on the sloppy ground. He lost his balance and slid down the side of the house. He kept his momentum going, scrambling forward on his hands and knees to get to cover. He didn't know it, but his opportune fall saved his life from the sniper's bullet. It punctured the air where his heart would have been a split second before.

He finally made it to the front of the house. Inside the landscaping, in front of the porch, he flipped up a rock in the flower bed and grabbed the spare key from its hiding spot. He jumped onto the porch and let himself into the house. He rushed quickly through the doorframe, not stopping until his back was up against the far wall of the dining room, right next to his mom's prized china, proudly displayed in the china cabinet that was providing some cover on his left side.

He crouched down and held his breath, listening for any sound that would betray the presence of any threats. After an eternity, which lasted about three beats, he stood and rushed down the entry hall, into the kitchen. He wasn't happy that his father's deep voice failed to challenge his entry. His mother's voice didn't call out to him either. The light filtering into the room gave him enough to see that he was alone. He strained his ears to pick up any sound. The house felt empty. His lungs screamed for oxygen. He fought the urge to breathe and strained to hear any sound that would give away the presence of an intruder. He let his breath out slowly and silently made his way around the first floor of the home he grew up in. Nothing looked out of place. He knew there was a threat. What he didn't know yet, was if the threat was in here with him, as well as out there in the dark.

After making sure the ground floor was clear he made his way up the stairs as silently as possible. He knew the boards that creaked and avoided them. The upstairs was as empty as the ground floor. Without wasting any more time, he went into his parents' room and retrieved what he needed. It was hanging right where it had always been, fully loaded and ready for action. He took down the rifle and walked over to the window. He hadn't turned on any lights as he went through the house. There was no way his adversary, or more likely, make that plural, he thought, had seen him as he moved through the house. He closed the bedroom door so no hint of light could light up his silhouette. He peered out from the thin crack between the curtains into the darkness outside.

The floodlights on both ends of the barn lit up the area. Inside the barn, the lights were all on. He took a minute to wonder about what had been bothering him since he came into the house. His dad could be out there in the barn, but his mom almost never went out there. If she wasn't in the house, then, where was she?

Bill crossed to the window on the other side of the room and looked down at the police cruiser. Gonzales wasn't there. The doors were still wide open. He strained to see into the back seat of the cruiser. The shadows were too dark. He had no idea if the girls were still there. He watched the car for a few beats more. "Damn it," he muttered under his breath. Not so typical SNAFU. *Why isn't the dome light on?* He wonders. He knows it could be as simple as the bulb had burned out, or Gonzalez might have realized the light gave him away when he was flanking a position for a take-down. He tried to think back if the light came on when he opened his door and couldn't latch onto the memory.

He pushed his anxiety for his parents, and the girls away. There'd be time to worry later. Right now, he had to act. Stay still, and you die. It was a truth he'd been taught through hard-fought lessons. He forced himself to focus on what had to happen. All the time that this dialogue played out in his mind he methodically scanned the darkness for any signs of motion, any tell that would give away the shooter's position. He knew it was a long shot, but he had to try. He knew what he had to do.

Bill made his way back through the house and eased out into the raging storm.

He ran as hard as he could across the open expanse between the house and the barn, careful to keep out of the light cast from the floodlights on the outside of the barn. The storm had turned the yard into a mess of puddles and mud. He'd just come past the front of the barn when he saw a pick-up truck idling on the side of the barn. He planted his feet to stop his forward motion, sliding in the muddy mess.

"Shit!" he exclaimed. He was only twenty feet in front of the truck and still sliding in the mud when the headlights lit him up. He saw the surprise on the faces of the two men in the front seat. Their shock gave him the crucial second, he needed to dive out of the glaring lights.

He did a shoulder roll to get him even further away from the men in the truck. The puddle next to his head vomited forth a splash higher than the others. What may have been a crack of a gunshot shortly followed. It was hard to know for sure because the night was split with a loud peal of thunder from the raging storm.

Move! Move! Bill kept low and ran around to the back of the truck, hoping the men would continue to look for him where they last saw him. He knew speed was his ally in this fight, so he sprinted to the back of the barn, and slammed into, what he had a split second to realize was a man. His momentum carried him in the direction he was going, and he landed about three feet from the stunned look-out. The force of the impact knocked the rifle from his hands. The gun was lost in the darkness and the muck. Without giving it another thought, he settled for a kind of crab scramble back to the man. Speed was his friend. Any hesitation or doubt could cost him his life. He was on the man before he knew what he was going to do. His battle training was leading the way. He slid his body next to the man and forced his leg under him and wrapped his right arm around the man's neck, locking in the hold with his left. Using his legs, he arched his back, increasing the pressure on the man's neck, cutting off the air and blood flow. Bill knew that in a few seconds the man would pass out. Hopefully, it would happen before the guys from the truck come around the corner to check with their friend.

SNAFU!

"Let him go and back up, nice and slow."

Bill's mud-splattered face looked up into the bores of two pistols pointing right at him. He hesitated for a beat while weighing his slim options.

Fault Line©

The man who gave him the order stepped to his left to get a better bead on Bill's head.

"Last warning, amigo."

The calm tone that the warning was delivered in told Bill that this man was fully in control of the situation.

Bill raised his hands and scooted back from the man he'd choked out. The guy's head dropped into a puddle with his face turned to the side.

Bill didn't care whether he drowned or not, but he watched the reaction of the two men and saw that they didn't care either.

If there were only one guy, he would have taken a shot at overpowering him.

If the men had been standing closer together, he might have tried slinging mud into one of their faces and attacking the other.

The reality was that his best option was to follow the orders given him, bide his time, and hope an opportunity presented itself.

"Get up nice and slow. Keep your hands where I can see them," the taller of the two men said.

Bill complied, getting awkwardly to his feet.

"Now walk into the barn."

As soon as he entered the barn, he saw his father tied to the second support beam. He was standing with his legs spread and a defiant look on his weathered face. A bruise was already forming on his forehead, and a cut on his left cheek was oozing blood.

On the other side of the barn, Sebastian and Raul were tied to another beam. Raul was sitting on the floor, his chin resting on his chest. The dark stain encircling him was a bad sign. The familiar squeal of protest the stool at the workbench makes whenever his father sat down on it drew Bill's attention to the other side of the barn.

Tommy and Sam were secured to another one of the support beams. Tommy had been shot in the right leg. He was sitting down with his back to the beam. Bill couldn't see Sam clearly but judging by Tommy's thumbs up sign they must have been okay.

Fault Line©

"Why don't you tell me what you're doing here?" The man sitting casually on the stool was the same one he'd seen at *The Thorny Cactus*. He casually pointed a pistol at Bill.

"Just coming home after a night on the town. I thought I would have some dinner with my parents. Hey Dad, are you okay over there?"

"Doing fine Son. These men came by to ask you some questions. I guess they weren't satisfied with the answers your friends and I gave them."

"How are you, Sebastian?"

"Hey Bill, I'm good. I just wish they'd untie me. I would like to have a long discussion with these guys. You know, a man to man talk. I guess they're too scared though."

Two men were guarding the entrance to the barn by the big doors. The guys that had gotten the drop on him were standing on each side of the support beams his friends were tied to. They had the area covered with the exception of the back half of the barn behind them. With all the lights on, it was plain to see that no one was there.

The men were armed with what looked like Browning automatic rifles.

Bill was watching to see what the man's reaction would be. Not much was the answer. He knew Sebastian was trying to get under the men's skin. If they were angry, they might make a foolish mistake.

"How about Raul?" Bill asked.

"He's not good brother. He took one in the gut about forty-five minutes ago."

Bill took a couple of steps toward Raul before he was cut off by one of the guards. He looked over at the man in charge. "Come on man, let me check on him."

At a signal from the leader, the two guards took Bill, one on each arm, to the support nearest to his father and tied him to it.

While they were securing him, the man in charge got up from the stool and walked over to Raul. He knelt in front of him. Raul was taking shallow, rattling breaths. His skin was lighter than his usual color, and a sheen of perspiration covered him. The man reached out his left hand, the one without the gun, and lifted Raul's shirt. Satisfied with what he saw he stood and walked over to stand in front of Bill who was now securely tied to the thick support beam.

"It doesn't look good for your friend. It looks like it hit his liver." He paused to let that sink in. "If you tell me what I want to know, you might be able to get him to a doctor in time." His ice blue eyes peered into Bill's. They were taking each-other's measure. Neither man showed the slightest sign of backing down, not that either one expected the other to do so.

"Why are you and the other soldiers here? I already know you were part of the group that took away my girls. I am very unhappy about that."

"I'm a business man though. I know how to control my emotions. This is all about business, and you and your friends here have cost me a great deal of money. Okay, as you gringos like to say *Shit Happens*!" he said expansively, waving his gun around. "I know when it's time to go, amigo. I would just appreciate knowing how you found out about me. I'm a professional, my friend. I learn from failure. So, tell me why you're here, and we'll be on our way?"

Bill smiled. "It has nothing to do with you. I told my buddies that I was going back to see my family on their ranch. They thought that spending some time in the Lone Star State sounded like a good idea. Your man messed up our relaxing weekend when he went all berserk on Main Street. We just happened to get a coffee at the right place at the right time."

The man stared at Bill for a bit. His ice blue gaze looking for the truth. He stepped back from Bill and slowly walked around in a circle, his boots clunking on the wooden floor of the barn. He tapped the barrel of his pistol on his leg as he considered what Bill said. He stopped back in front of Bill and shook his head. "You know my friend, that's a good story. It sounds nice. It rings with the truth. It even waves the flag a bit. It is patriotic and makes me all nostalgic for that good old hometown feel. In fact, I believe you. It's too boring to be anything but the truth. I just don't think it's *all* of the story." He lowered his head and focused his gaze on the floor of the barn. He absent-mindedly tapped his gun against his jeans-clad thigh.

He focused his cold eyes back on Bill. "I need the whole story, my friend." He waited a couple of seconds.

When Bill didn't say anything, he tilted his head to the side. Kind of like a dog would do.

"I see you need motivation." He spun around in a fluid motion and shot Raul in the head.

"You son of a bitch! You're a dead man," raged Sebastian. He lunged forward straining against his bonds.

The man pivoted and in four quick strides was standing face to face with Sebastian's seething rage. "You're right my friend. I am a dead man. I've been a dead man for a long time now. I died on a dirt road in a town nobody knows about in a country that you Americans look down on. I was eleven years old when I died." The man didn't raise his voice or betray any hint of emotion while he said this. It was stated as a simple fact. "I am a ghost, and it is now my time to vanish."

He looked over at Bill. "Let's try this one more time. Why are you here?" he asked as he brought his pistol up to Sebastian's forehead.

What happened next took place in the span of less than six seconds. The glass in the window on the west side of the barn blew in. Miguel's face jerked to his right as if he'd taken a punch to the side of his head. The force of the blow knocked him to the floor.

Sebastian broke free of his bonds and ran across the dirt floor. He went for the pistol that had been flung from Miguel's fingers, dropping to his right knee he slid across the remaining distance to the pistol. He snatched it up and brought it up to his line of sight while still sliding across the floor.

Miguel had almost made it out into the stormy darkness when Sebastian had him in his sights. He managed to squeeze off four rounds before Miguel cleared the door. The two guys who were guarding the door abandoned their post when they saw their boss making his escape.

Sebastian spun around and shifted his sights to the two other targets. The men recovered from their surprise. They were bringing their rifles up to bear. Sebastian hit the man closest to him in the leg then shifted his sights to the second target. He squeezed off three rapid shots to center mass. The man did a jerky dance and then crumbled to the floor. Before the dead body landed, he tracked his weapon back to the man he wounded.

He was just in time. The guy was clasping his leg with his left hand and was bringing up the rifle with the other hand.

"Hold IT!" Sebastian yelled at him. "Just drop it, and you won't die."

The man had the weapon up to his waist, the barrel still pointing down at a forty-degree angle.

A Novel by T. L. Scott

Sebastian had his head resting stock still on the front sight. Sebastian's attention was so focused he actually saw the man's right eye squint down a split second before his right arm flexed and began to bring the barrel of the rifle up.

He squeezed the trigger of the fully automatic weapon, pumping hot lead out of the barrel. Two rounds managed to escape before the slug from Sebastian's pistol entered his head, just above his left eyebrow. The next slug caught him in the left cheek, below the orbital bone. The third round missed him. This was probably because he was falling back and to his right from the force of the high-velocity rounds entering his head. The rifle spat out another six rounds before his lead scrambled brain directed an impulse throughout his body to flex his extremities. His trigger finger straightened with such force it was cut on the trigger guard, not that it made any difference, he was already dead.

With both immediate threats neutralized, Sebastian trained his sights back onto the entrance to the barn. The one that the leader had fled out of.

"You okay, Bill?" He asked as he trained the weapon across the open space.

"Yeah, brother. The shot that came through the window came from somewhere, be careful."

"Thanks, brother," replied Sebastian as he closed the distance to the barn door. He looked out and, not seeing any immediate threats, went out fast. He turned to the left and ran around the edge of the barn. The taillights of the departing truck were rapidly receding down the driveway.

Something set off his alarms. He whipped around. A man in a police uniform faced him from about twenty feet away. He held his pistol in one hand, the other one he held out, palm up toward him.

"Take it easy now," the cop said to him. "I'm Deputy Gonzales. We met at the station earlier."

Sebastian had already recognized the man but wasn't taking any chances. He didn't know who's side this man was playing on. He wasn't going to make a fatal assumption just based on a uniform and a badge. He knew that corruption crossed all kinds of lines.

"Are you the one that took that shot?" Asked Sebastian.

"Yeah, I tried to hit him when he came out of the barn. I think I may have clipped him when he ran for the truck," he replied.

"Did you see anybody else out here?" Sebastian asked him. He'd been asking about the shot through the window and noted the disconnect.

"No, the two guards at the door jumped into the truck before I could get a shot off. The last one out, I'm pretty sure I clipped him. He hopped into the passenger seat, and they took off. You should know there were two people in the back seat of the truck. I think it was the girls we came here with. Is Bill okay?" He asked.

Fault Line©

"Let's go inside and talk with him," Sebastian said, flicking the pistol toward the door of the barn.

Gonzalez noted that the man hadn't holstered his weapon. He wasn't taking any chances, and he didn't blame him.

Bill had untied his father, and they were both working on freeing Tommy and Sam. Hearing the men come into the barn Bill pivoted on his foot, seeing who it was he lowered his weapon. He saw Sebastian look over at Raul and then back to him. He knew the question that Sebastian was asking, so he shook his head; Raul was gone. The rifles from the two men were propped against the support that Raul had been tied to.

Gonzales updated them on what he had seen since he had come to. "I woke up looking at rain splashing in a puddle and the underside of the car. I sat up and saw that the car door was still open. My chest felt like I'd been hit by Thor's hammer. The body armor did its job, but it still hurt like hell. The girls weren't in the back seat. I grabbed the shotgun and made for the shadows."

"When I came around the back of the barn, I saw the guard standing between the truck and the front door on the other side. I made my way around so I could look in through the side window. Before I could get there, that man came running out of the front.

"Hey, Dave," said Bill's dad. "Come on in from the rain, son."

Everyone turned to look at the man standing in the side door of the barn. Dave was an imposing man. He stood six feet six and took up most of the space inside the door frame.

Bill crossed the barn and walked over to his old friend. "Thank you for taking the shot, Dave."

"I think I missed." He said as he looked around for the body.

"No brother, you got him. I'm afraid that the rain and glass deflected your shot a little though. He was able to get away."

"I tried to stop the truck as it drove away. I might've got him then," Dave said hopefully.

Fault Line©

"When I saw that guy take his shot," he said as his eyes darted over toward Raul's body, "I knew I had to do something. I tried to keep the men from leaving. Two guys ran to the truck first. I tried to shoot in front of them. You know, to scare them from getting into the truck. It didn't work though. One of the guys started shooting back at me. When your shooter came out the front, I was already shooting at his friend. Like I said, I think I hit him."

"Jorge, do you have any idea where they might be going?"

"I wish I did. I've been thinking about it, and nothing stands out."

"I might have an idea."

The men pivoted as one towards the voice.

"Agent Cavanaugh!" he announced. "Stand down gentlemen."

The men visibly relaxed having recognized who had joined them.

"We were close by when we heard the gunfire. As we were crossing the field between the warehouse and here we saw a vehicle, it looked like a truck, leave here. It went about two miles down the road and then turned right. It didn't travel much farther before it stopped. Is there something down that way?" Mike asked.

Bill's dad answered him. "Yeah, that's the Hobbs place. Nobody's lived there for a couple of years though. He finally packed it in and has been leasing out the land."

Mike was nodding his head and looking at Deputy Gonzalez. He noticed the shredded front of the deputy's uniform and the small cuts on his face. "Are you okay deputy?"

"I'm good," Gonzalez responded.

"Agent Cavanaugh was it?" Bill's dad asked.

"Yes sir," he answered with a nod of his head.

"What was going on over at the Jensen warehouse?"

"I don't want to go too much into it, but," he looked around at the men, "we found more people that this gang had locked up. We also recovered a lot of drugs and managed to capture some of the gang. There's no doubt that these are the same people involved with the house we took down earlier."

"So, are some of your team with you, here?" asked Bill's dad.

"Yes sir, they're guarding the perimeter."

"Yeah, that was pretty much what I figured, but I wanted to be sure." He turned and walked over to the phone mounted on the wall. He picked it up and punched three digits into it. "Hi honey, it's all clear up here. Come on out." He hung the phone back up in its cradle and then turned back to the men. "I'm going to go in the house and fix a drink. The offer is open, but I expect that you gentlemen have a bit more work to do. Better get to it too. The sun'll be up in a little while." He looked at each man in turn, finally resting on his son's face. He gave a small tilt of his head and then turned toward the house.

Bill met his dad half-way to the door and the men embraced in a hug. Bill could feel his dad was tense. His muscles were taught and his back was rigidly straight. They held the hug for a moment until his dad took a small step back and brought his hands up to his son's shoulders.

"Tell mom I'll see her in a little while for some breakfast."

"I sure will son. I'll ask her to make those biscuits you like."

"Thanks, Dad."

Fault Line©

Chapter 16

Mike planned on encircling the ranch and closing the trap before the gang had a chance to flee. Bill, Sebastian, Sam, and three uniformed officers were making their way across the saturated ground. They were responsible for assaulting the farm from the rear. The plan was to catch the gang in a wedge and force them to escape from the front of the property. Mike would be waiting for them. He already had tire killers strewn across the driveway.

His team was staggered in four sets of four. Depending on how many vehicles attempted to escape they would converge on the disabled vehicles in groups of four, two, or if there were three then only one person per team per vehicle with one hanging back for cover. If there were four or more vehicles, then Mike planned for them to stay in teams of four and close their escape off with his men scattered along the line of disabled vehicles.

A Novel by T. L. Scott

Bill squinted his eyes to see through the rain. His face stung from being pelted by the falling deluge. The fat rain drops exploded on impact with the ground, casting a fine mist into the already saturated air. So much water was in the air that it was making it hard to breathe. Every ragged breath felt like he was breathing through a wet towel. His lungs felt like they were filling up.

Progress was reduced to an agonizingly determined shuffle. Each step was an effort to stay upright. The sucking mud frustrated their need to move with speed. With each step, he strained to pull his boot out of the muck and maintain his balance. They had to be on time to meet up with the other elements of this impromptu strike team for the assault to work.

Bill had the radio and was listening to the progress of the other teams through the Bluetooth earpiece looped around his ear. He continually updated his mental picture of the terrain as they reported in over the net to Mike. It was clear the other teams were also finding the conditions as challenging as his team was.

Fault Line©

The storm provided the cover they needed, but it was also seriously impeding their progress. He feared that by the time they got into place, Isabella and Izzy would be out of their reach. He tried to pick up his pace as a bolt of lightning lanced across the early morning sky. The thunder crashed down on them from the oppressive darkness. Bill looked over his shoulder and stopped.

"What's up?" asked Sebastian as he scanned the area looking for a threat he missed.

"We need to move brother," he replied. "We're about to get slammed."

The men watched as lightning lanced along the tower of clouds barreling down on them.

The main section of the massive storm had arrived. Up to this point, they'd been dealing with the effects of the fringe of the hurricane.

"Mike, we've got some nasty weather about to hit us," he reported in over the radio.

"Shit! I was hoping it would have turned east before now. It's the remnants from Hurricane Beatrice. How long do you estimate before it hits us?"

"Not more than fifteen minutes. Maybe less than ten. It's hard to tell how fast the wind is pushing it."

"How far are you guys from the objective?" Mike asked.

"About a half mile, maybe less."

"Copy," Mike replied.

"Mike this is red team. We copied last and are about the same distance out."

"Understood. We're in position at the front. Nothing new to update you with here."

Bill looked behind him and saw a wall of darkness fleetingly broken by flashes of lightning tearing across the massive storm front bearing down on them. All the men increased their efforts.

"Aw shit, this is the last thing we need right now," declared Sebastian. The men had come to the bank of a stream. Water rushed along the steep banks. The engorged stream was only about six or seven feet wide. Normally, each of the men wouldn't have a problem crossing this barrier. The rushing water and the steep, slippery banks made fording the stream tricky at best. The simplest way to cross it was to jump over it. The problem with that was the slippery ground. Getting enough speed to propel them across was doubtful and added to that was the very real possibility of slipping on the launch.

These men were used to solving problems on the go, and this was just another problem to be solved. Sam positioned himself on his hands and knees as close to the bank as he dared.

"Ready?" Bill asked.

"Will you move your skinny ass already?" answered Sam.

Bill was back about thirty feet from Sam and the edge of the stream. He needed to get enough speed to clear the distance. As he expected the first few feet were lost to slipping and sliding. He was able to find a rhythm to his feet sliding in the mud. By the time he got to Sam, he had thought he was moving fast enough. He jumped up and launched off Sam's back. The force of Bill's speed made Sam unexpectedly slide towards the water. Bill wasn't ready for it and didn't get as much height as he had planned. Fortunately, his momentum and the added height he had gained from launching off his back, carried him to the other side. He landed safely with a couple of feet to spare. Then slipped and sprawled on his ass. He turned his mud-splattered face to the left and shouted, "Come on, move it!"

Sam adjusted his position a foot farther away from the edge and dug his fingers and boots as deep into the ground as he could. He then braced himself for the next man. All he was able to see was darker shadows rushing towards him out of the night. He prepared for the impact of the men launching themselves off his back as much as possible. Even so, he was sliding towards the bank of the rushing stream. After each man he scrambled back into position, balancing a fine line between being too close and too far away from the edge.

On the other side, Bill was up on his feet. He was catching the men in his arms as they landed, feet scrambling in the muck for purchase, in an attempt to steady them as much as possible. He looked across the void and watched the last man run towards Sam.

"Oh fuck!" Bill groaned. The man slipped a couple of steps away from Sam. There was no way for him to arrest his momentum. Sam saw what was about to happen and tried to get out of the way. There was no time. The man slammed into Sam, tumbling both of them into the raging waters.

Bill sprinted along the bank, his hands fumbling to undo his belt. Timing his jump, he landed on his stomach, sliding out over the edge of the bank. His left hand dragging through the muck for anything to grab onto. Hoping that at least the drag would prevent him from falling into the water as well. Disregarding his own safety, he reached his right hand out as far as he could. The tip of the belt danced on the surface of the surging water. He strained his eyes, scanning for a sign of the two men. His chest and shoulders hung out over the water. He was arching his back, trying to dig his boots and knees into the mud for leverage. He felt a hand grasp his left leg, arresting his forward momentum. Just then his right arm jerked hard to the right. The force pulled him to the side so far that half his body was suspended over the water. All he could see was a head breaking the surface of the water and a hand holding onto the belt. Trusting the men to hold onto him he strained to stretch out his left hand so he could grasp the belt in both hands. He strained his eyes for a sign of the second man in the water.

He felt himself being pulled back onto the ground. He held onto the slippery leather of the belt with all he had. If he slipped, it would be the man's death. Seeing the man clear the bank, Bill craned his head to see if the other man was holding on to his leg. There wasn't anyone there.

Fault Line©

Exhausted he dropped his head and lay on his side to try and catch his breath. The air was so heavy with water he wasn't getting enough air into his heaving lungs. Panting, he rolled onto his hands and knees to give him some free space. It felt like he was in a shower. The shower heads spraying at him from all directions. Once he was able to get a good breath, he turned his head to look at the man they had pulled from the water. Sebastian was lying on his back fighting to recover. One of the other men was using his body to block the rain from his face. The other two men were out of sight.

They regrouped to the area where they had crossed the stream. They had all dropped their gear when they saw the men fall into the water and were now putting it back on. They found no sign of the man that went in with Sebastian.

"Mike, it's Bill here, copy?"

"Go, Bill, are you guys in position?"

"Negative. We lost a man crossing a stream." He paused a minute before going on. "We're on the move again and should be in position within ten minutes."

"Copy, Bill. All other teams are in position. Nothing has changed here."

"Roger that, Mike. I'll report in when we're ready."

The storm was raging all around them. Bill estimated the wind was blowing at around thirty knots. Fortunately for them, it was mostly blowing at their backs. The rain was blowing almost horizontally. It hit them so hard that it stung where it hit bare skin.

The rest of the journey was uneventful. Bill decided to fan the men out fifty feet apart from each other. He didn't want these men to escape again. He had a bad feeling that if this didn't end here, then there wouldn't be another chance to save Isabella and the little girl.

Fault Line©

Chapter 17

The light from the overhead lamp cast a yellow hue over the dingy kitchen. Years of accumulated smoking and cooking with less than attentive cleaning had left their mark. A residue coated every surface. The odors made the air feel thick with years of frustrated living.

The linoleum was so worn out that whatever colors and patterns that had been there weren't discernable. The only thing it conveyed was a sense of being utterly tired. The old Frigidaire in the corner was performing admirably since it had to be at least fifty years old.

The room was a mess of beer cans, dirty dishes, and trash of all varieties covering every surface. The floor was littered with bloody gauze around where Isabella was working to close Miguel's wounds.

"Are you done yet?" Miguel asked her with an edge of frustration that hadn't been there just a few minutes ago. He was straddling the plastic seat, hands gripping the thin chrome frame of the seat back.

"Almost there," she told him. She had already sutured the wound in his side and was almost done with the last one in his shoulder. She'd taken as long as she thought she could stretch it, in the hopes of Bill catching them here. When they had first arrived, this man had brought Izzy upstairs and stayed up there for a few minutes with her. Isabella was surprised to see that he obviously cared for the child.

"I'm going to put in a couple of cross stitches, and then I'll be done here." She told him.

"About damn time," he grumbled.

"You don't want them to open back up, again do you?" she asked him.

"What, these little scratches? Honey, I've had much worse, and I'm still here."

Fault Line©

Miguel talked with his men in Spanish while Isabella finished up. She didn't know if he thought she didn't speak Spanish or if he didn't care if she overheard. If he didn't care, then she was in real trouble. No, she corrected herself, either way, she was in real trouble. She let go of the fantasy of these men letting her go. She was either going to become one of their prisoners or she would be killed to keep her quiet. Unless she was rescued.

"She's your daughter, isn't she?" She felt his muscles tense as he sat up straighter in the chair. "I see the way that you are around her. She's special to you."

Miguel turned in his chair and looked directly into her brown eyes. "She means a lot to me. The only reason you're still alive is because she likes you. You make her feel safer. If anything happens to her, it is going to get really bad for you."

Isabella did not avert her gaze from those arctic blue eyes. She did not see anything but sincerity in them as he explained her worth to him.

A Novel by T. L. Scott

Miguel stood up and took his shirt off the counter. He held it up. "This won't do," he declared, looking at the blood-soaked material with holes punched through it.

"Vamanos! Dos Minutos," he pronounced as he went upstairs to look for a shirt and to get Izzy.

Chapter 18

"Do we have eyes on the girls?" asked Mike over the radio.

"The woman is still in the kitchen. The little girl is upstairs, ... wait, I have movement. One of the men is moving through the living room."

Several seconds passed while Mike listened to dead air. He felt time slipping by as if it was a physical thing.

"Everybody stay chill. I have movement on the front left curtain."

What felt like five minutes passed. It could have been as little as two. It felt like time was stretching. They had to spring the trap, but his instincts were telling him that this was not the time.

"Okay, he's moving upstairs."

"What are these bastards doing?" Kat asked Mike.

A Novel by T. L. Scott

"I don't know. I never thought they'd stay here this long. They must feel pretty safe. It makes me nervous. I expected them to bug out pretty fast."

"Agent Cavanaugh, Bill here." Came over the radio.

"Go ahead, Bill," he responded.

"We're still holding for a bit, right?" he asked.

"Yeah, what are you thinking?"

"I'm going to disable their vehicles." He went on to explain his plan to Mike.

"Go ahead, but keep your ass down Sergeant."

"Yes, sir. I've grown rather fond of it."

Bill cut across the distance from where he'd been holed up at the edge of the corral to the back of the house. Sebastian was following behind, watching his back in case there was a sentry they hadn't spotted.

They made it across the open ground without incident. The storm was providing them as much cover as it was impeding their movements. The wind had continued to pick up strength. It was now blowing at least forty knots. They had to lean into it to make forward progress. The gusts were strong enough to rock them back on their heels and caused them to slide backward. The ground was so saturated that it wasn't soaking up any more water. The pools of water were already several inches deep.

Having made it to the relative safety of the side of the house the men rested for a minute with their backs pressed up against the back wall. To Bill's best guess, they were leaning against the outside wall of the pantry, so there was minimal chance anyone had heard whatever sound they might have made. After catching their breath, Bill crouched down and began making his way to the corner of the house. He strained his ears to catch any sound that the enemy might be making. It was impossible to tell with the storm raging around them.

They could see the back quarter-panel of a dark-colored pickup, parked about ten feet from the side of the house. Bill looked back over his shoulder and gave

Sebastian a nod of his head. Keeping low he launched himself across the empty space between the house and the truck.

And came face to face with Raul's killer. From the look on the man's face, he was just as surprised as Bill. Bill held his fire. Something held him back from sighting in on the man he was after. His instincts were fine-tuned, and he knew better than to think in situations like this. He was in battle mode and was responding to more than what his conscious mind was processing.

There was a reason he hadn't dropped the hammer yet. He saw the man lunge back into the house and then violently jerk backward. Isabella was yanked from the house by her arm. She planted her feet on the threshold of the door and propelled herself back into the house.

The man lost his grip on her rain-slicked skin and stumbled back into the cab of the truck.

Fault Line©

Bill shifted his weight and planted his right foot down to stop the momentum of his slide. His boot found little purchase in the muddy, rain-soaked drive.

Sebastian came out from the side of the house high, as planned, and seeing their primary target scrambling into the open truck door didn't hesitate to engage.

Glass from the back window of the cab shattered as the truck roared to life. Gravel and mud shot out from its big wheels as they spun for purchase. Back into action, Bill lunged forward and reached for Isabella's hand.

She reeled back from the mud splattered form that was coming at her from the shadows.

"Isabella, it's me, Bill," he said, closing the distance between them. He reached out to take her hand. She must have recognized his voice because she let him. He quickly led her to the other vehicle.

Bill looked back at her and was shocked to see her holding tight to Izzy's small hand, as they dashed for the dark Jeep Cherokee parked on the far side of the driveway. Isabella flung open the rear door and dove into the backseat of the SUV, dragging Izzy in right behind her. Conveniently the keys were in the ignition, so Bill wasted no time. He gunned the big V8 engine to life, and they were in pursuit of the fleeing enemy. Izzy barely got her feet inside when the tires found traction, slamming the door closed as the Jeep leaped forward.

Bill was torn between getting the girls away from the danger of this place and chasing after a crazy killer during a hurricane. Neither option was appealing. *Well it's only the edge of the storm so we should be okay*, he reasoned. Decision made, he turned the wheel to the right. The Jeep lurched hard as it left the gravel drive. It bucked like crazy over the uneven ground. Izzy screamed from the back seat as she was launched into the air. Bill let up on the gas.

"Seatbelts," he commanded, scrambling to get his on with one hand and fight the muddy terrain for control with the other. He strained his ears for the sound of the belts clicking in over the loud tattoo of the storm pounding on the skin of the SUV. Eager to not lose sight of the fleeing tail lights, he forced himself to wait. He had the wipers on their fastest setting, and they were barely making a difference. The red lights had faded to a dim glow.

"We're in," responded Isabella.

Bill stomped down on the pedal and felt the off-road vehicle lose its footing in the muck.

He eased up on the gas so the Jeep could do as it was designed to do, and that was to get them through this mess. The big tires caught and propelled them forward. He cursed the weather and the way that it was slowing them down. He was only able to keep the Jeep at a frustrating twenty miles an hour. He took solace in the fact that they had made up a little of the distance between them.

They crested a rise, and Bill realized he had lost sight of the lights. He strained his eyes to re-acquire them. After thirty seconds of frustrating efforts, he reached down and cut the headlights. He slowed them down to a mere crawl, hoping he'd be able to spot them. He scanned the horizon, taking one section at a time. He moved his eyes along in a grid pattern.

"Bill, look, over there to the right," said Isabella pointing to the two o'clock position.

He saw the far away glint of red, that she was pointing at and realized they had separated about thirty degrees from each other. The truck must have turned right while he was cresting the rise. He corrected his heading and pressed down as hard on the accelerator as he dared.

He felt, more than saw, the water they were plowing through. There was more resistance to the tires forward progress. Something from the corner of his eye caught his attention. A quick glance brought their situation into focus. The dim light of the false dawn cast enough light to see the stream he had crossed earlier. The raging waters had breached its banks, and the field they were cutting through was quickly flooding. *So, this was the reason the truck had turned right.*

Fault Line©

Bill cut the wheel and fought to keep clear of the path of the flood waters. Fortunately, they were almost to the road. The Jeep easily crossed the remaining distance. As soon as the tires hit the asphalt, Bill cranked the wheel to the left and stomped the accelerator to the floor.

"Bill, can you hear me? Bill are you there?"

He took his eyes off the road long enough to glance down at the passenger seat. In his rush to follow the fleeing truck, he must have tossed the radio there. With all the bouncing around it had fallen onto the floorboard. He heard Mike's tinny voice coming from the speaker. It was barely loud enough to hear over the staccato roar of the rain as it pelted the exterior of the Jeep.

"Isabella, can you climb up here? The radio is on the floor and I can't reach it."

She gave Izzy a reassuring hug then released her seatbelt and climbed into the front seat.

"Here, I'll hold it for you, just talk," she said holding the radio up for him.

Bill nodded his head and stole a glance at her.

She keyed the radio.

"I'm here Mike. I've got Isabella and the little girl with me. We're following the leader of the gang. He's back on SR47 heading east into town."

"Got it, Bill. Don't engage. Back off and keep an eye on him if you can."

Bill gripped the steering wheel hard. His knuckles turned white from his frustration. He wanted to get this guy, but he also knew that he had to keep his passengers safe.

They were driving east into the rising sun. Not that they could see much of it as the day dawned. The towering storm clouds had blotted out everything. The only sign of the beginning of the new day was an almost imperceptible lightening of the sky behind them. Their new path gave them a clear view of the towering storm clouds barreling down on them from the south-east. The vast power of nature's fury is fully on display to Isabella as she looked out the window. She reached into the back seat with her left arm and took hold of Izzy's hand. She felt the girl's grip tighten, seeking comfort.

The road they were on led back into town in another four miles. Bill wondered why the man would be going into town instead of trying to get away. As much as he wanted to catch the man who killed his friend he made a snap decision.

"Hold on!" he shouted, then stood on the brakes before cranking the wheel to the left.

"Why are we going here, Bill?" Isabella asked him.

"I want you both safe, and the only place I know where that will be is right here. There's a storm cellar under the house. Well, it's a bit more than just a storm cellar. Dad fixed it up to be more like a hardened bunker. You'll both be safe from the storm and from anyone trying to get in."

Isabella looked over at him. He could tell she had more to say on this but was holding her tongue, for now.

She held the little girl's hand and gave it a comfortable squeeze. "You hear that sweetie? Bill has a really nice safe place where we can go."

"You'll love it," Bill joined in. "My mom has all kinds of games and toys down there. She even has movies to watch. It'll be fun," he assured her.

He brought the Jeep to a stop in the muck by the door to the house. He kept his hands on top of the steering wheel, knowing his dad had been watching the strange Jeep speed up to his house.

Bill opened the door, keeping his hands in plain view, unsure whether his father could see his face. He saw the curtains flick back into place in the kitchen before the door opened a crack. After a second it opened all the way, and his mother waved them into the house, out of the rain. Once the girls were safely inside, Bill looked back down the drive. He didn't see any other cars coming after them. Satisfied he went inside his childhood home.

"Where's dad?" he asked his mother.

Fault Line©

"He's gone back down into the shelter. You know him, always making sure it's ready for us. It looks like we will be down there for most of the day. The forecast is pretty rough. Even if we get lucky and the storm breaks east, it's going to be a mess out there."

"Mom, I can't stay. I still have some business to take care of."

She didn't say anything. She simply raised an eyebrow. It was a look he had come to know well over the years. It said that she knew there was more to say. The look practically screamed the question, "So, tell me why you are back here then if there is someplace you need to get to."

"Can the ladies join you to weather out the storm?" he asked her.

"Of course, they can," she declared. "In fact, I'm happy to have the help. I'm going to make some cookies and I need a couple of hands. I also need someone to tell me if they are any good." She looked at Izzy. "Do you like cookies?"

Izzy nodded her head that she did.

"Do you like chocolate chip cookies?" she asked the little girl.

Izzy nodded her head a little bit quicker, and a grin began to curl up the corner of her mouth.

"Well, then it's settled. We can make the cookies together and later we can play some games. It'll be fun," she replied.

"I'll be back as soon as I can mom. Maybe the storm will pass and I'll be back sooner than we think," he said looking at Isabella.

"I'm going with you," she stated firmly.

Bill looked at her and saw the determination set firmly in place. Still, he had to try to keep her safe.

"Don't you think it'll be fun making cookies with Izzy and my mom?"

Isabella feels the little girls hand squeeze hers. She squeezes her own hand in response and then shakes it back and forth. "Of course, I would, silly," she said looking at Bill. "But then who would keep you out of trouble?" she asked raising her voice on the last word. She looked down at Izzy and rolled her eyes dramatically. "Boys sure are silly. They are always getting themselves into messes."

Bills mother didn't miss a beat. She knew what Isabella was trying to do. "Don't even get me started on how big of a job that is," she exclaimed. "He's always getting into some kind of mischief." She put her arm around the little girl's shoulders and lead her gently into the kitchen.

"I remember this one time when Bill was, oh about eight or so when…," Izzy looked back over her shoulder.

Isabella and Bill both gave her a reassuring smile. Isabella also gave her a small wave of her hand.

Bill's mom went on telling her story, as she led the little girl away from them and into the kitchen. Bill could tell that Izzy wasn't completely sold on the idea of being separated from them but was resigned to go with his mother.

A Novel by T. L. Scott

"You should really stay too," Bill said. Turning to look Isabella full in the face. "I know you don't want to. I can see that you aren't going to, but I have to tell you that this isn't over yet. I wasn't planning on leaving Izzy, but I had a strong urge to come here. The closer we got to the drive the stronger the urge became. I trust my instincts."

Isabella met his gaze without flinching. Nothing in the set of her face or her body language indicated any sign of backing down.

He let out a long sigh. "Last chance," he said hopefully.

Isabella slowly shook her head. "I'm seeing this through."

"Why? Why are you so determined? I know you're tough, but that isn't the reason you are doing this. Why do you need to see this through?" he asked her.

She looked at him for so long without answering that he was about to ask her again. She turned away and looked down at her hands.

Fault Line©

Bill followed her eyes. Her hands were clasped together so tightly her fingers were turning white from the force. She took a deep breath and slowly let it out again.

"I told you that I was here to write a story about the hardships of undocumented aliens." She looked up at him. "I am. I'm a freelance writer, and I think the story is an important one. It needs to be told. It's just not the whole reason I'm here. When my little sister, Amanda, was sixteen she started running with a bad crowd and got messed up with drugs. She dropped out of school and was coming home less and less. I was away at college, so I didn't know how far she'd fallen. I came home for Christmas break that year and did what I could to get her out of that life. We had some hard talks and lots of tears. I was able to get through to her. I took off the next semester to focus on her. My parents were supportive too, but my sister never listened to them."

Bill saw the smile light up her face even though her eyes were still far away.

"Excuse me," said Bill's mother. She came into the room and handed a wet cloth to Isabella. She then squeezed her upper arm before turning and walking back into the kitchen.

Isabella put the cloth to use cleaning the mud off Bill's face while she went on with her story.

"Amanda was always a stubborn rebel. She had to go her own way. She wouldn't just color outside of the lines, she'd draw a whole other picture and color that the way she saw it. She wasn't mean. She was just stubborn. She was a good girl who was trying to find her way." She paused and took a couple of breaths while she collected her thoughts.

"By the end of the summer, she was ready to go back and finish high school. I went back to school too. Things were going well. She was concentrating on school and staying clean. When I came home for Christmas break, she looked really good. She was smiling again. She was happy. She had just started working a job after school a few nights a week as a waitress." She paused in her story to collect herself.

She had finished cleaning his face and was now working on cleaning his arms. The cloth was beyond dirty, so she was really just smearing the mud around. Neither one of them was really focused on how clean he was getting. Bill was struggling to focus on her story and not be distracted by the energy he felt from her touch.

"I got a call in February from my mom," she said, continuing her story. "She told me Amanda had started hanging out with her friends again. We were both worried that she would fall back into trouble. We also both acknowledged that she was a teen and needed to have normal social interactions. She needed good friends. Fortunately, I was coming home in two weeks for spring break. We would be able to talk then."

Bill saw a tear fall from her eye. She absently wiped it away and took a shuddering breath before continuing her story. "She disappeared on a Tuesday, February 23rd. My parents filed a missing person report, but the police didn't take it very seriously. She was seventeen, and with her history they expected her to come back soon. They didn't tell me about it until I got home. They didn't want me to leave early and miss any more school if it was nothing. It wasn't nothing. She's still gone."

"I talked with her new friends and started following the threads. It has taken me almost ten years, but I know now that I have been right. I've tracked her trail and people have said that they recognize her from the pictures I showed around. And then I lost the trail about four years ago."

"Nobody recognized her picture anymore when I showed it around. I decided to go back to the last town where someone recognized her. That's when I got an unexpected break. I showed a bartender a picture of her at a party. It was a picture that one of her friends back home gave me. The person didn't recognize her. She recognized a man that was standing off to the side of her though. A man with piercing blue eyes that contrasted with his jet-black hair and dark skin. She said that his name was Miguel. Not much to go on but it was another lead for me to pull on."

"When I was in Texas a few years ago, I made friends with an ATF agent who recognized Miguel from his picture. He was a man that the ATF and Border Patrol and a lot of other agencies were looking for. Miguel Menendez was a known operator. He was wanted for drug smuggling, arms dealing, human trafficking, prostitution, and the disappearance of several people. My friend was able to search through some official files and found several pictures of my sister with Miguel."

"I followed the trail through New Mexico and back to here, in Texas. This seems to be the area he likes to operate out of the most. I haven't had any more sightings of my sister, but Miguel I'm able to track. Now I know I made the right choice to continue following him."

After waiting for an explanation, Bill had to ask. "Why do you know now that you made the right choice? Have you seen her? Is she here?"

"No, I don't think she's here, but I believe her daughter is. I'm sure Izzy is Amanda's daughter, and Miguel is the father." She could see the doubt cross his face. "The resemblance to my sister is just too strong to deny. You heard Izzy herself say that Miguel treats her differently. I don't think she knows he's her father, but she does know that he looks out for her."

"Listen, I know you want this to be true, and I'm not saying that it's not, but you have to admit the odds are that she isn't your niece, right?" Bill didn't want to tell her that he had noted the resemblance between Isabella and Izzy earlier. If they weren't related, then this was a big coincidence unless Miguel had a penchant for a certain type of woman for himself. A type that matched Isabella's missing sister. The more he thought it over, the more the odds were in favor that Izzy was her niece. Either way, it didn't matter right now. What mattered was trying to find this Miguel.

"We need to go back to the police station," he said shutting the Jeep's door. "They are the only ones that may have an idea where he's gone," he told her, putting the Jeep into drive.

"What about going back and talking with that FBI agent? He said he's been watching Miguel for a while. He probably knows where he's going," She reasoned.

Bill had to admit that she was probably right. Cavanaugh was probably their best chance of catching Miguel. He decided to turn right, back to the ranch next door, instead of left to the police station in town. As they reached the end of the drive, a parade of dark SUV's and squad cars went tearing past them, heading into town. As soon as the last car passed them, Bill pulled out and fell in behind them. Something else was going down, and he wasn't going to miss it.

A Novel by T. L. Scott

Chapter 19

"Jorge, I hope you are almost here. It doesn't look good."

"I need you to keep calm, Thomas. You're safe in there. You know that room is reinforced. I need you to tell me what's going on." Jorge kept his voice calm as he talked with his officer over the police radio from his car.

"They came in so fast, Jorge. They came in shooting," Thomas said as he took in a ragged breath. He couldn't take his eyes from the lifeless arm. He knew it was Sgt Janson by the charm bracelet on her wrist. After they had stormed through, he watched in horror as her fingers twitched. He was transfixed watching her. It seemed to take forever for her to lose her fight with death.

He was recording everything digitally. He was also keeping a written record of what he witnessed as well, including this conversation. It had happened at 6:38 AM.

Fault Line©

Everyone was getting ready for shift change. The change would have been only a formality. Most of the reliefs had been on the response team since yesterday. There just wasn't anyone that wasn't already on the clock. Overtime had been authorized, and the small law enforcement force was approaching 24 hours on the clock.

Sergeant Rodriguez was in charge of the station. She was down checking on the prisoners when five men stormed in. They had their faces covered in baklava's so identification would be difficult. Their intention was clear. They wanted their friends released.

The security cameras throughout the station were always recording. Their feed was sent to the unit in the control room Thomas was manning. It was also sent off-site to a backup recorder. As soon as he saw the masked men, Thomas turned on the microphones in the interrogation rooms. He didn't expect to get much off of them, but he knew they needed as much information recorded as possible.

A Novel by T. L. Scott

The men came in fast and, once, inside the station, they spread out. Janson panicked and started to scream. One of the men walked over to her. He just stood in front of her, watching her.

Thomas listened to Janson begging them not to kill her over his headset. The man didn't speak a word. Or, if he did, Thomas didn't hear him. He watched the man raise his gun and shoot her in the chest. He displayed no emotion as he watched her fall. He stood there and just kept looking at her. Thomas couldn't see any more of her than her hand and part of her forearm. That was enough for him. Those twitching fingers would haunt his nightmares for the rest of his life.

The two men that had come in first grabbed Santos and shoved him toward the hallway. The one that went past the door Thomas was hiding behind. They stopped and checked the door. Finding it locked they didn't waste time on it. Thomas watched them as they looked into each of the interrogation rooms. Satisfied they were empty, the man signaled for the rest of them to follow him. He held up at the top of the stairs that led down to the basement and the holding cells. They forced Santos to go down first.

Rodriguez had nowhere to go. She had her revolver in her trembling hands. A thin sheen of sweat coated her skin. Her breath was coming in rapid gasps. She watched as a pair of shoes, black patent leather, then tan uniformed pants, came into view. *Shit, they're using him as a shield*, she thought.

Santos had enough presence of mind to drop and roll down the last few steps.

Rodriguez took advantage of the change and charged the stairs. She engaged the invaders. One of the men was on the left side and about halfway down the steps when she shot him just above the right knee. He'd been stepping down with his left foot. The man jerked back, falling into the man who'd been following close behind him. Rodriguez raised her sights and put two rounds into the other man's side. Seeing no more obvious targets, she ducked to the side and used the wall for cover.

The other men fled back up the stairs. Santos was able to wrestle away the weapon from one of the men, and in the process the gun discharged, killing the man Rodriguez had shot in the leg.

Thomas watched helplessly as the men regrouped at the top of the stairs. The microphones were only able to pick up a few of their words. He could tell that they were speaking in Spanish. He'd lived here long enough to pick up some of the language, but he wasn't good at it. He was able to understand enough to know they were making a plan for assaulting the cells without getting their friends killed. Two of the men searched the station looking for another set of keys.

The key box was locked and mounted to the wall. Out of frustration one of the men opened fire on it. This only made holes in it. Another man came over and hit him in the head. He probably told him that he was being stupid. The keys inside were probably toast. They don't hold up too well to bullets.

Santos had stationed himself near the bottom of the stairs. He was keeping his eyes up to see anyone coming down, as soon as possible. Firepower poured down from above catching him by surprise. He wasn't in the direct path of their sights, but it was a small space and bullets ricochet. He took slugs in both legs and went down hard. The bullets didn't stop coming. They poured a steady torrent of lead down the stairwell. They must have shot a few hundred rounds before they finally let up. After half a minute, one of them cautiously climbed down the bullet-riddled stairwell. He kept his back to the wall and crouched low, trying to see below the basement ceiling as soon as possible. When no shots sounded two other men started to follow him down as well.

The first man down saw the body of the cop lying about six feet from the bottom of the stairs. He split his attention from him to scanning the space. The men they were trying to free were in two cells on the right, four in the second one, and three in the third one at the back. The cells on the left looked empty. He paused at the bottom of the stairs. He looked to his left, straining to see as much of that cell as he could. There was a mattress rolled up on the empty bunk, so he was confident it was empty. He threw himself to the other side and trained his gun on the last cell. It was in the same condition as the one on the left.

His attention went back to the body of the cop on the floor. His blood was mixing with the blood of his two brothers who were lying just past him. His brothers in the cells were yelling and pointing at him. Misunderstanding what they were saying he thought they were cheering him on. Shooting guns in small spaces is definitely not good for your ears.

He walked over to the body of the police officer and started looking for the keys to the cells. While he was doing that, his friends had made it to the bottom of the stairs, and seeing no danger, went over to the cells.

Fault Line©

Rodriguez was pressed up against the wall, as far under the bunk in cell one as she could be. When the man kneeled down and started rifling through Santos's pockets. She was scared he would see her. She didn't realize she'd been holding her breath until spots began to pop in her vision. She slowly let it out. She struggled to keep her hands from shaking and kept her sights trained on the man. She was about to squeeze the trigger the rest of the way when she saw movement at the bottom of the stairs. Easing her finger off the trigger by a couple of ounces of pressure she waited for the new targets to come closer.

She had only seconds until their confusion cleared and they figured out where she was. She had a clear shot at two of the men, but the third was blocked by the kneeling man. The dull roar of voices was starting to resolve into discernable words. She knew the time to act was now. If she didn't engage the enemy now, she was dead.

A Novel by T. L. Scott

Bracing her shooting hand as much as she could while lying on her side in the cramped space under the bunk, she applied the remaining pressure and let her training take over. She shot the kneeling man twice; center mass then shifted her sights to the next target and fired four more shots. The third target went streaking past her toward the steps.

She rolled out from under the bunk and swung her weapon in the direction he had fled. Seeing nothing, she rose to a kneeling position and quickly scanned the area. A man inside cell three was reaching for a gun. She shot off two rounds close to his grasping fingers. He pulled his hand back inside the locked cell and held his hands up, palms out. Movement out of the corner of her eye made her pivot back towards the stairwell in time to see a body fall to the floor.

She had no idea what had just happened. She backed up to the end of the hallway and pressed her back up against the wall. She positioned herself so that she had maximum visibility of the space in front of her. Two of the prisoners were injured from the barrage of gunfire that had poured down on Santos.

She slid down the wall into a sitting position, resting her shooting arm on her right knee to give it better stability. She fought to get her breathing under control and steady herself. There was no way for her to know what was going to come at her next. All she knew was that she had seven more rounds loaded in her weapon and two more clips. She was good for now.

"Sergeant Gonzales, this is Thomas."

"We're almost there, Thomas. ETA is two minutes. What's the situation?"

"Unless there are more outside, I think we're clear here. Santos and Janson are down. I don't know what the status of Adams is. I think Rodriguez is okay."

"Are you still secure, Thomas?"

"I'm locked in again. I saw one of them coming back up from the cells and engaged him, then locked myself back in."

"Good work, Thomas. We're pulling up now. Keep your eyes open. I don't see anyone else out here but give us a minute to clear the area. I'll let you know before any of us try to enter. Where's Rodriguez?" he asked.

"She's down guarding the prisoners. I have eyes on her. She's backed up against the wall at the end of the hallway."

"Alright Thomas, good work. Just hold tight for a few more minutes."

It took them another fifteen minutes to ensure the station was clear. They found Adams behind his desk. He had been shot before he had a chance to clear his weapon from the holster.

Fault Line©

Chapter 20

It was taking every ounce of self-control for Miguel to not kill the human waste sitting in front of him. He was thinking of many satisfying ways to end this man's life as he went on and on about how it wasn't his fault.

"How was I supposed to know of a secret operation? This wasn't even talked about in any of my men's briefings. It had to have been totally black."

"You have to understand. I can't go around asking too many questions. It'd look suspicious. I have to keep my distance from this stuff. I have other work to do too. I can't ignore those things. I have to let others do the detail stuff. I must rely on them to tell me what is going on after all."

Hearing enough, Miguel leaned forward, closing the space between them to an intimate few inches. "I have been paying you very good money for you to keep our arrangement. You have never failed to accept my money. You didn't feel the need to keep any distance from my money. In fact, for a long time now you have been doing little more than just taking my money."

The senator sat back in his chair, trying to put as much distance as possible from the piercing gaze of this man. "That's not fair, Miguel. I've influenced the situation to keep the police from looking at your operations too closely. I've also kept you informed of any sweeps that were going down before they did."

Miguel stood up to his full height of five nine and spread his well-muscled arms out from his sides. "But here we are today, my friend. I have lost my whole operation here. I've lost my brothers. They are dead because you didn't tell me about these fucking soldiers. Why are they here at the same time that the FBI is here? Don't you think that is just a little bit curious?"

"It's just a coincidence. That soldier's sister really is getting married. They've been planning it for over a year. I didn't hear anything about the FBI investigation.

My sources didn't pick up anything about it. I don't know how it got past them. I'll get to the bottom of it."

"It's your son that's getting married to her. You knew she had a brother that was a soldier and was going to be at the wedding."

"I didn't know he was bringing friends with him. Miguel, it's not like I was involved in planning the guest list. I don't even talk with my ex-wife. My son and I don't even talk very much anymore."

"I want the names of those sources," he said, locking his blue eyes intently on the soft face of the senator.

"I can't tell you who they are. We need them in place. They trust me."

"Senator let me make things very clear for you. Someone was either incompetent and let this happen, or they were complicit and helped to make this happen. In either case, they cannot be allowed to get away with it. I can't believe that it's just a coincidence that the FBI and a group of highly trained soldiers just happened to be in town when we are trying to move this shipment through."

"Now, now don't even try," Miguel said, raising his hands to forestall the protests he knew were coming. "I know you're going to try and talk your way out of this. You are very good at talking. It's one of the reasons I chose you. Your sources are yours. It's true. I respect that. I have my own sources and appreciate that you need to take care of them. The thing you need to know, right now, is that you are the one that is responsible for your sources. Your sources that failed to inform you that this shit-storm was coming. In other words, Senator, you failed to inform me."

The sweat freely ran down the chalky colored skin of the old senator's face. He was desperately trying to think of an angle out of this. "You can't just kill me," he stated, unaware of the whiny note of his voice. "It'll bring even more attention to this. You don't need any more attention. We need to let this situation die down. Once things blow over you can set up operations somewhere else."

"You know, you're right," agreed Miguel. "We do need to let the dust settle for a while, and we will set up in another place. But don't you think if we set up in your jurisdiction again it'll be just a little obvious? Don't you think that this ass-fuck of a day we've had won't cause all those agencies with letters for names to be watching this area very closely? So, tell me, what use you are to me?"

"I can still watch out for you. You know I've given you useful information."

"Yes, but don't you think I have others who do the same? You don't think you are the only dirty, money-hungry American do you?"

"You are right that if I were to just kill you and leave you here, it would be bad. There would be way too much publicity. The problems, so far, will fade from the news in a couple of days. You know how you Americans need to have the latest news. But a senator wrapped up in this scandal? That would lead to much more publicity than I need. Hell, the news trucks would be arriving here in a long parade and almost double the population of this shitty place before the sun went down tonight. No Senator, you are going to be caught in a scandal of another type altogether. I'm thinking you are going to disappear for a few days and then you'll be found in a rat hole hotel dead from a drug overdose. I may make it even more interesting and have you lying next to a dead prostitute. It would be poetic considering how badly you've fucked me over."

"Miguel, come on. Can't we work something out? Can't we talk about this?"

"I'm done talking." Miguel stood up from his chair and struck out, so fast Senator Camacho didn't know what hit him. One second he was sitting at the table, the next he was lying on the dirty concrete floor.

"Pick up this piece of shit," Miguel told his men. "You know what to do with him."

Fault Line©

"Miguel! You can't do this! I'm a fucking United States Senator! You can't just kill me!"

"You're just a man. You'll die like any other," Miguel said as he walked out of the building.

A Novel by T. L. Scott

Chapter 21

With things at the station in hand, Bill and Isabella didn't have any direction to go. Miguel wasn't there. If he wasn't already in the wind, then he had gone to ground. Either way, they weren't likely to find him by waiting at the police station. So they made a plan to go and get Isabella's things, then head back to Bill's parent's place.

"So, there was just you and your sister growing up," Bill asked her.

"Amanda is four years younger than me. I was always her big sister. Four years is a pretty big gap when you're young. She started acting out when she was about ten. Our parents were the quiet type. Dad worked at the bank and mom took care of the house. They really didn't know how to deal with the strong personality she started to develop."

"Was she acting out to get their attention," Bill asked her.

"I guess that was part of it. I think she was trying to get my attention too. By then I was interested in hanging out with my friends." Isabella went quiet for a little bit as she got lost in her thoughts.

The song playing on the radio was interrupted by a loud beeping sound.

This is a tornado warning. You should take shelter at once. Funnel clouds have been sighted, and suspected tornados have been reported. This is a tornado warning….

The weather warning repeated itself a few more times.

Bill looked over at Isabella. "We'll be quick right?"

"I'll be in and out in less than five minutes."

They both turned their eyes up to the stormy skies. The rain was still coming down. It had eased up a little from the earlier downpours, but it was still coming down strong. At least they could see where they were going.

True to her word Isabella was back in the Jeep in no time at all.

"You weren't joking were you," he asked her.

"I never really settled in. I kind of live out of my bag," she said with a shrug of her shoulders. "I've learned the advantages of being able to grab and go." She told him.

This is a tornado warning. If you are hearing this, you need to take shelter immediately. A confirmed tornado sighting was reported one-mile northeast of state road 118.

"Okay, we'll be at my folk's place in just a couple of minutes. Then we can relax in their shelter. They even have a shower down there. I don't know about you, but I sure could use one."

"A hot shower sounds —"

She didn't get the chance to finish what she was saying. They were hit hard from behind. The Jeep skidded around, its tires stuttering in protest. It ended up facing the way they had been coming from. Bill found himself looking at Miguel. They were separated by only a few feet between the two vehicles. It was such a shock he almost didn't react in time to the sight of the pistol barrel coming to bear on him. Without thinking about it, he leaned forward and slammed his foot down hard on the accelerator. The Jeep lurched forward.

Bill quickly cut his eyes away from the road and looked over at Isabella. "Are you hit," he asked her.

"No. How the hell did he find us?"

"I have no idea. I didn't see him coming."

They were driving away from his parent's house and out of town. He knew this area like the back of his hand, having grown up here. He knew that in two miles if he took a right, he could circle back around to his parents. He also knew that a half mile before that turn there was a smaller road that led back into town. He might be able to lose him on that road. There were some sharp turns, and if he did it just right, he might be able to lose him long enough to get away.

Just then the driver side mirror shattered. Bill felt a small punch to the Jeep. "Get down," he shouted. He slid down in the seat as far as he dared.

"He's shooting at us," he called out to her.

This wasn't going to work. Bill needed to see how much Miguel had closed the distance between them. He risked reaching his hand up to the rearview mirror. "Shit," he cursed under his breath.

Isabella was looking at him. Fear clearly written on her lovely face.

Bill didn't want to lie to her. "He's getting close."

"How close, Bill," she asked.

"Less than fifty feet," he told her.

The back window of the Jeep was punched with three holes in quick succession. Bill instinctively crouched down lower hearing the crunch of the slugs punching through. He expected them to go through the windshield too or at the least to cause it to crack. To his surprise, nothing happened to the windshield. He wondered briefly where the bullets had gone. Realizing he hadn't been looking at the road he was racing down, he risked sitting up a little in favor of crashing into something.

Fault Line©

A flash of light caught his attention a split second before Miguel rammed his truck into the back of the Jeep again. Bill fought for control on the slick road. The tires broke free and lost their grip a couple of times. Bill steered into the skid and was able to manhandle it back under control. He pressed the pedal down all the way to the floor again.

"Bill, can you go any faster?" asked Isabella.

"I've already got it floored. I can't go any faster. It'll take him a little bit before he closes on us again," he said trying to reassure her.

"Have you seen the radio? We need to let Mike know what's going on. Maybe we can lead him into a trap," Bill said.

"I've got it," she declared after a little while searching for it. "It was lodged between the door and the seat."

"Okay, can you make sure it's still on channel eight?"

He glanced over at her. She was focused on the radio and looked a little less scared. He was definitely glad for that.

"Got it," she told him.

"Good. Let him know we're traveling . . . On second thought, please just key it and hold it up so he can hear me."

"Agent Cavanaugh, are you there, over?"

After about ten seconds they got a response. "Go for Cavanaugh."

"Agent Cavanaugh, this is Bill. We're driving east on SR 47 with Miguel Menendez chasing us. I'm going to cut back towards town on County Road 1142. That's going to place us on Ranch Road 23 heading southwest. Do you think you could get some help in place about a mile out of town? We'll be there in about five minutes."

"We've got bigger trouble than Miguel," Isabella informed him.

Bill risked a look behind them. His foot eased off the accelerator. His attention was riveted on the dark funnel cloud barreling down on them from their right side.

He'd been so focused on keeping the Jeep on the road and not getting shot that he hadn't paid attention to the sound that was getting louder by the second. It sounded like a train engine barreling towards them.

His head was snapped forward. Miguel slammed the truck into the back of the Jeep again. Bill didn't hesitate, he stomped back down on the gas pedal. They had to be nearing that turn-off, he figured. If he could make the turn to the right, he could get them out of the path of the tornado. Then again, he didn't think Miguel was going to give them time to slow down for the turn.

He leaned forward, straining his eyes to see the road. They had to be getting close.

"It's almost on us, Bill. Can't we go any faster?" she asked him. Isabella was practically yelling at him to be heard above the roaring noise of the wind. Bill could feel the winds buffeting the Jeep. Debris was hitting the jeep, powered by the high winds. He wasn't sure if it was real or just his imagination, but it felt like they were slowing down. It felt like the twister was sucking them in. He was already gripping the wheel so hard his knuckles were white. He pressed his foot down harder on the accelerator. It didn't matter. It was already down to the floor.

The noise in the jeep was overwhelming. It felt like the passenger side was being used for target practice. The twister was ripping through the cornfield. The stalks and ears of corn were smashing into the vehicle, propelled by the high winds. The rear, side windows exploded, the glass flying around inside the vehicle. Bill slammed on the brakes and leaned over, trying to cover Isabella with his body.

After what felt like an eternity the noise faded away. They were alive. The jeep had come to rest on its side. Bill reached up and positioned the rearview mirror to look behind them. He didn't see Miguel or the tornado. Isabella began to stir. She flung her arms out in a panic.

"It's okay, we're okay," he reassured her.

She looked around, taking in their situation. Her breathing settled a little.

"Push down on my shoulder. Take some of the weight off of the seatbelt so you can release it," he told her.

"Okay," she said.

Bill was ready for her weight and helped ease her down.

They walked out of the back window. It had been completely knocked out at some point. They stood looking at the vehicle. It had really taken a beating. A stalk of corn was standing up from the passenger side of the rear quarter panel. It had been impaled into the metal by the high winds.

They stood looking at the destroyed vehicle. After a couple of minutes, Bill realized the engine was still running. He went back inside and turned it off. When he came back out, he saw that Isabella had turned her attention to what was around them.

A Novel by T. L. Scott

The cornfield on the left side of the road looked like a giant combine had mowed through the field. The twister had passed over the road, right behind them, and began to churn through the field on the left side. The path of destruction tapered in width and stopped a short distance away.

Bill reached out and took Isabella's hand in his. They stood looking at the destruction for a few minutes, trying to take it all in. Bill had been here before. He'd been left standing after facing impossible situations. He knew that there was no single reason for it and trying to sort it all out was impossible.

He squeezed her hand a little to pull her attention back. "Come on," he said to her.

She didn't ask him where. She walked with him along the path of devastation. The tornado had paralleled the road for a couple of miles, staying about a quarter mile away until the end when it took a sharp turn to the northwest and crossed the road before going back up into the sky.

Fault Line©

They walked a little over a mile. They were looking for any sign of the truck Miguel was driving. A farm house was about two miles away, set back from the road on the right. He might have veered off his pursuit and tried to hide there and ride it out.

A trio of vehicles met them about a half mile from the farm house. They were the team Mike had sent to intercept Miguel. The search of the farmhouse came up empty. The family that lived there had been in their tornado shelter, so they hadn't seen anything.

They didn't see any sign of the truck. It wasn't lying on the side of the road. They didn't even see any sign of the truck crashing. It was too much to hope that he'd been swept away by the twister.

It was just as likely that he had left the road and cut across a field to avoid the tornado and figured they weren't worth risking his life for anymore, except they didn't see any signs of a truck making a mad dash through the crops.

A Novel by T. L. Scott

Bill knew from experience that sometimes things just happened. There was no right or wrong to it. As the saying goes: Shit happens!

Fault Line©

Chapter 22

It turned out that three tornados had touched down. The largest one was evaluated as an F4. Bill and Isabella had barely avoided being killed by it. The tornado had crossed the road right behind them and continued to track north-west for about a quarter of a mile more before dissipating. They had been just far enough ahead of the swirling vortex that their forward momentum, and the diverging track of the twister, allowed them to avoid being sucked into the devastating winds.

They found the truck Miguel had been driving. It had been picked up by the twister and tossed into a field. The truck had flipped over side to side for an added 250 feet from where it had landed. The roof was crumpled all the way down to the tops of the doors. All of the windows had been blasted out.

There was a significant amount of blood on the driver's seat and the steering wheel, but no body. He could have been sucked out of the cab and thrown clear of the wreckage. His body could have also been tossed clear while it was flipping through the field, buffeted by the tornado. It could also be buried under the mud somewhere in the field. The fact was that without a body, there was no way to know for sure what had happened to him. Without a body, they had to assume he was still alive and still a threat.

After the events of the past few days, a significant federal law enforcement presence descended on the town. They had taken custody of the truck, and the forensics team was cataloging everything they found. They had Miguel's blood, fingerprints, hair, and skin samples on file now. If he was still alive, it was going to be easier to track him.

The news networks had descended on the small town in force. The story had gone national, and updates were still getting top attention. Most of the major networks and some of the smaller ones were still hanging around. News of a senator being killed in a storm was too juicy for them to miss. Bill had been harassed by several of the journalists, so he had taken shelter at the ranch. It was private property, so the news crews were forced to camp out at the end of the long driveway.

Agent Cavanaugh and Kat were still in town as well. Mike had relinquished authority to the local head of the station and was very happy to do so. He loved being a field agent but dealing with the press and politicians was not his thing.

Julie and Tom postponed the wedding a couple of days. His father hadn't been seen since the day before the storm. His secretary said that he left his office around noon on Friday and looked like he was in a hurry. That wasn't anything out of the ordinary. Senator Camacho was always in a hurry. He was a busy man, and it wasn't unusual for him to rush out for meetings throughout the day. His secretary kept his schedule and confirmed that he hadn't had any meetings scheduled for that afternoon.

A Novel by T. L. Scott

He usually took his lunch and would often conduct meetings at the country club. He didn't dine there on Friday. The hostess that was on shift during the lunch hour stated it was kind of busy. People wanted to get out before the storm rolled in. She said that she knew the senator as he was a regular and always left her a big tip for getting him the table he wanted. He didn't come in to dine on Friday. She was certain that he hadn't come into the bar either. She had a clear view of the bar from her podium, and he would have had to walk right past her to go in. The senator hadn't been seen at any of the other restaurants in town. One motorist came forward to say that he saw the senator at a stoplight heading out of town. That was the last time anyone saw Senator Camacho.

He was one of eight people that were unaccounted for. The death toll so far was at fourteen confirmed dead. A family of four had tried to cross a flooded road. Their SUV was found three miles downstream. Judging by the damage it had been rolled several times. All four were still inside wearing their safety belts. A forty-three-year-old man, coming home from work, was killed when an old tree fell in front of his car. He didn't have any time to react. He'd been creeping along at only thirty miles an hour due to the low visibility. The three-thousand-pound vehicle hit the tree with so much force the branches of the old oak impaled the car, relocating the engine block into the passenger compartment. Another branch had gone through the windshield on the driver's side. He never had a chance.

The tornados destroyed eighteen homes. Most of the fatalities from the storm were in two of the homes. One family had been hiding in their downstairs bathroom. It was the safest room in their house. The family of four were all taking cover in the bathtub, both parents and their three and five-year-old daughters. They had a mattress draped over the top of them. When the tornado struck their home, the father was reading a story to them by the light of their flashlight. The twister ripped into the side of the house, completely tearing away the south wall and most of the east as well. Without their support, the top floor and attic came crashing down. The load bearing wall on the far side of the bathroom collapsed under the force of the crashing debris. If it had fallen on top of them, they might have survived. It would likely have fallen on the side of the bathtub and could have provided protection from what was crashing down from above. It fell the other way. The floor above them partially collapsed causing the furniture in the master bedroom to come sliding down. The massive hand-crafted armoire, that the wife had been so happy to buy at an auction in the spring, landed in the bathtub, crushing everyone.

The other family was taking shelter in their storm cellar. Their house also collapsed on top of them. The debris of their home blocked the escape door. They couldn't climb out, but the shelter was strong and withstood the assault. Unfortunately for them, a couple of things occurred which, on their own, would not have been a problem. But they did interact, making their already precarious situation worse. The force of the falling debris broke the main water pipe. It also shifted the ventilation shaft which fed fresh air into the storm cellar. The water from the pipe initially had no place to go. The force of it gushing out quickly eroded the ground around the break. The water then did what it does. It followed the path of least resistance. In this case, it flooded into the break at the top of the ventilation shaft and poured into the storm cellar. The family did everything they could to try and stop the water from pouring in. The father managed to tear the ventilation shaft off the wall in the hope of cutting off the flood. It only increased the rate of flow. By the time the neighbors were able to clear away enough of the debris to get to them, it was too late.

A Novel by T. L. Scott

Chapter 23

Bill was sitting on the back porch steps with his little sister Julie next to him. They were enjoying a quiet cup of coffee, not saying anything, just content to watch nature's glory. The few clouds on the horizon were lit up with the rising dawn. The screen door opened and was eased back shut behind them. The old boards of the porch tracked the light tread of their mother to the porch swing which hangs on the north side. The chains rattled as she eased onto the old cushion. Five minutes or so passed without anyone saying a word. William joined Maria on the porch swing. The family sat in a comfortable silence, content to watch the beauty of the rising day.

After a little while, things would become very hectic. There were a multitude of tasks still to be accomplished and a magnitude more that would need to be managed. It was Julie's wedding day.

Fault Line©

Tom insisted on proceeding with the ceremony in-spite-of the uncertainty of his father's fate. He was sure that his dad wouldn't want them to hold things up because of him. There still was no sign of him. None of the hospitals within a hundred miles had anyone matching his description, and there were no new unidentified persons by the police either. No one would ever know for sure what became of the Senator. He was presumed dead as a result of the storm even though his car was never found.

The arrival of a beat-up Chevy pickup interrupted their solitude. The truck barely came to a stop before Sara jumped out. "Good morning," she called out, waving her hand in greeting.

Julie put her hand on Bill's knee and gave it a squeeze as she stood up. She met Sara at the bottom of the steps and gave her a big hug.

"Well, honey, the first thing we need to do is fix that bed head you got goin' on," teased Sara. The day was officially underway.

Maria leaned into William and gave him a kiss on his stubbly cheek. "I better go and watch over them. You okay, old man?" she asked him, tilting her head a little to the side.

"I'll be okay, momma. I've had twenty-three years to get ready for this."

She squeezed his hand before getting off the swing.

Bill kept on sitting on the step. The sun had cleared the horizon and was rising into the few clouds that dotted the sky. It was looking like it was going to be a really nice day. He was thinking about how strange it was that in a few hours his baby sister would be married. He was remembering some of the things they had shared doing when the firm grip of his father's hand on his shoulder brought him out of his reverie.

"She's going to be okay, son," he said as he sat down beside him.

"I know Dad. She's always known how to take care of herself. It's not her I'm worried about. I wonder if Tom has any idea what he's in for."

His dad chuckled and shook his head. "I 'spect not, son. I don't think any man really has any idea until years later. By then it's much too late."

"Tom's a good man," he went on. "I'm sure he'll take good care of her. It's a shame about his father though. I don't really like the man. He smiles too much. I always feel like he's working a deal. I don't really trust him, but he's done well for himself. Tom seems to have inherited that hard-working trait. He'll take good care of Julie," he said again. Bill was pretty sure he was still trying to convince himself that it was true.

A Novel by T. L. Scott

Chapter 24

Julie's white train flowed out behind her, sliding along the white runner, her twin cousins holding the end of it. Tom's niece and nephew led the wedding procession down the aisle. She was four and doing an excellent job of spreading the rose petals everywhere. He walked as serious as a six-year-old could, stiffly pacing out the walk just as he had practiced all morning.

The assembled guests were all in their places on each side of the aisle. There were just under two hundred people in attendance. The large tarps that had been draped over the damaged sections of the church gently flapped in the breeze.

Bill was standing at the front of the assembly as one of the groomsmen. He was two guys away from Tom. From his place at the front, he watched his father's rigid demeanor. His dad never liked being at the center of attention. Bill saw that the gravity of the ceremony was weighing on him. It was one of a father's greatest honors and one of his most difficult duties. Handing over one of the most precious things in the world to him. A person he has cherished and protected up until the moment when he literally hands over that duty to a younger man.

The nervous groom was standing by the preacher with a big grin on his face. His eyes were fixed on the vision that was his bride-to-be walking towards him. Everyone was in their place.

It was a beautiful day. The temperature a comfortable eighty-two. Only a few puffy clouds languidly made their way across the clear blue sky. A light, fresh breeze was coming in from the south-east. The air felt clean after the storm.

Movement to his left drew Bills attention. A crow landed upon the roots of the tree lying mostly inside the church. The bird hopped among the gnarly old roots. He knew it was probably searching for a meal. For some reason, the sight of the crow gave him a bad feeling. He brought his attention back to the ceremony.

Julie looked beautiful in her dress. She had just made it to the front of the assembly and taken her place by her bride's maids, facing her groom. His dad raised her veil and kissed her on the cheek. He stayed there for an extra beat as he whispered something in her ear. He stepped back, still holding her hands in his and took a long look at his little girl. He nodded his head and placed his daughter's hand in Tom's. He nodded his head to Tom then turned and walked slowly to his seat. Julie and Tom turned to face the priest. She stumbled forward and fell into Tom's arms.

"Get a doctor!" Tom's deep voice bellowed out. A murmur rolled through the crowd.

"Is she okay? Did she faint?" The questions rolled over the crowd.

"She's been shot. Call 911!" Tom yelled out.

People were looking at each other, wondering what to do, then they heard the last part of what Tom said and they scrambled for cover. Most of them headed to the church to take cover there. Others ran for their cars. What had been an orderly scene had been torn apart.

Bill knelt by her side. He looked down at her white dress as the red bloom grew in size. He swallowed the lump in his throat and with it the anger. She had been knocked forward, so the bullet had to have come from somewhere behind her. Since she was bleeding in front as well, the bullet had gone right through her and had probably not hit any bone.

Her eyes grew wide and her breath started to become labored, with a liquid sounding rattle.

He didn't know at what point he had held onto her hand. He gave it a reassuring squeeze and shifted his gaze to Tom.

"Tom, listen to me," Bill said firmly. "Put your hand here, and here." He instructed, guiding Tom's hands over Julie's wound on her back and chest. "Now, apply pressure. That'll help to slow the bleeding." He then gently rolled Julie into Tom's embrace. "Hold her to you. If it went through her lung, it will fill up with blood. We want the good one up, so she can still breathe." He looked Tom in the eyes. "Tom, do you have this?" he asked. Bill could see the terror and shock on the man's face. He also saw the determination.

"I've got her." Tom looked down into Julie's ashen face. "I've got you, baby, hold on. The doctor is on the way."

She smiled up at him, and he felt her squeeze the back of his arm.

"It's not so bad, babe. I thought I was just being clumsy and tripped." She coughed, and a little bit of blood sprayed from her lips.

"Don't talk sweetie. Just take it easy. I've got you," he told her as a tear slid down his cheek.

Bill knew he couldn't do anything more for his sister, for now, so he shifted his focus to where the shot had come from. He scanned the hill and any buildings where the shooter could have been hiding, straining his eyes to catch any sign of movement. He was surprised more shots hadn't come. They were out in the open and completely unprotected. He knew this had been a personal message to him.

Mike was talking on his cell phone.

Bill was sure he was coordinating a response. He looked over at Jorge and saw that he was doing the same on his hand-held radio. In a very short time, law enforcement officers would be scouring the area. He knew it would be too little too late. The shooter had taken his shot and had bugged out. He was gone in the wind.

They found where the shooter had set up at. It had been a very long shot, over 800 meters. Whoever had done this had been a professional. Bill knew it was Miguel. If he hadn't been the one to pull the trigger, he was the one that set it up. This had been personal. Miguel knew this would hurt him deeply. His sister had been the reason he had come home. She was the reason he was here. She was the reason Bill and his friends had been here to mess up Miguel's operations.

Bill looked up from the magazine he had been reading. There wasn't much of a selection to begin with in the waiting area. After all the time he had spent waiting for Julie to come out of surgery he had exhausted the little supply there was.

He looked up, sensing someone approaching down the hall. It was Agent Cavanaugh and Kat. Bill stood up to greet them.

"I heard she's doing really well," said Mike.

"She's a real fighter. I still can't believe that once she came around after surgery, she insisted on finishing the ceremony. She had the priest marry them right there in the recovery room," Bill responded shaking his head. "She was very lucky. The doctor said the bullet barely missed her heart. The funny thing is she said that she was distracted by the crow. Did you see it?" he asked him.

Agent Cavanaugh shook his head. "No, I didn't see it. She told me the story though. She said she was staring at it and suddenly, her legs went weak, and she started to fall. Then it felt as if she had been punched in the back. She swears to it happening in that order."

"Do you think he'll be back for her?" Bill asked him.

"I don't think so. I believe he wanted to send you a message. Even if he didn't get his full message across, he managed to tell you that he can take away what you care about. That will be enough. He's going to be busy trying to get set up in a new place. Unless his bosses take him out for this failure, that is. I hate to say it, but I hope he stays in play. At least we know to look for him. If they take him out, then we're at the beginning all over again."

Mike had personally called General Jones at Fort Hood and briefed him on what had happened and what role the soldiers had played. The Army claimed Raul's remains from the coroner and arranged a military transport to escort them home with honors. The guy's left the day after the wedding to escort him home. Bill planned to meet them there tomorrow for the funeral service.

"So, when do you think you'll be able to make it home again?" Isabella asked Bill.

"I'm never sure, but I'm going to try to come back in the spring. I've got to go back to complete this deployment. I still have fourteen months to go until my enlistment is up. I've been thinking about getting out of the Army for a while now. After this, I think that I'll look more seriously into some other options. What do you plan on doing?" he asked her.

"They tell me it's still going to be a few days until they know the results of the DNA test. I'm sure she's my niece, but it has to be official."

"Where do you think you'll go once all of the legal stuff is done?"

"Probably back to Phoenix. I'll need some help with Izzy. I know my mom will be more than ready to help take care of her."

"You're not going to stop looking for her, are you?"

"I can't, Bill. I still feel like she's out there," she said as she was looking down at the ground. She shook her head from side to side a little. "I'm not sure why I think so, but I just do."

"Have you ever thought about using those detective skills of yours on more of an official basis?"

"What do you mean?" she asked him.

"Think about this, if you were to join the Border Patrol or Homeland Security, you would have access to more information. You might be able to find a lead that others aren't interested in."

"I don't think so, Bill. I wouldn't be able to focus all my energies on finding her. There would be other cases. I don't want to lose my focus."

"You said yourself that you lost the trail before and had to talk to that friend in the ATF. You know they have good intel. Just something to think about, okay?"

"Yeah, okay. Thanks, Bill."

Now it was Bill's turn to look at the ground. He couldn't meet her gaze. "You know, it looks like we both have some free time tonight. Would you like to have a couple of drinks with me?"

"I'd like that a lot, Bill. As long as you promise to dance with me again."

He looked up at her and knew he was lost. A smile flitted at the corners of his mouth. "That sounds really good."

"Plus, you still owe me that game of pool."

Chapter 25

"Where is she, Miguel?"

"I told you, I lost her."

"Yeah, I got that part." The woman said with a sharp edge to her raspy voice. "I heard you tell me how you managed to escape but left our daughter behind. Do you have any idea who that woman was?"

"Just some bitch that got in the way," he told her. He knew that this was the woman that had been tracking them for the past couple of years. He was sure she was Amanda's sister. The last thing Miguel wanted was a family reunion. He had been grooming Amanda for years. She was now in charge of a critical part of his operation. He had learned early on that she was good with numbers. He allowed her to have increasingly more access to information about his network. She had developed spreadsheets to keep track of the complicated distribution lines which kept his merchandise moving. She had a real knack for it. Because of her, shipments had become more efficient, and the merchandise was arriving on schedule.

She knew he traded in guns and drugs. He kept her away from the other sides of his business dealings and used codes to hide what the merchandise really was. In return, he kept her addictions well-fed. He didn't love her. He wasn't capable of love. Miguel was a borderline sociopath. His emotions ran in a very small arc. What drove him was what people could offer him. Her body was still beautiful, and he took pleasure from it whenever and however he wanted. When she wasn't stoned out of her mind, she was really smart too. For now, she served his purposes. She may even prove more useful as a bargaining chip for little Isabella. He didn't love the little girl either, but she was his, and he meant to get her back.

The End

Fault Line©

The victims in this story are fictional, but human trafficking is real. There are an estimated 20.9 million people trapped in some form of human slavery today according to End Slavery Now.

This problem is a problem for all countries. America is not exempt. There is human trafficking right here, in the land of the free. People are enslaved right now. They are being subjected to cruelty and are being denied their fundamental human rights. Know the signs to watch for. Know what to do if you suspect someone is in danger. Help save a life. You can make a difference.

http://www.endslaverynow.org

https://humantraffickinghotline.org/states

https://www.state.gov/documents/organization/258876.pdf

https://www.dhs.gov/blue-campaign/what-human-trafficking

Know the signs.

Don't look the other way.

Save a life.

A Novel by T. L. Scott

His debut novel A Life Worth Living is the story of Dave, a husband, and father who makes sacrifices for his family. He works hard so he can provide for them. He sacrifices his time with them to provide them the life he didn't have growing up. When tragedy strikes, he is forced to decide how much he is willing to sacrifice to make his A Life Worth Living.

Available on Amazon, Barnes & Noble, and Kobo

Follow TL Scott

https://tlscotttheauthor.blogspot.com/

@TLScottAuthor

Fault Line©

T. L. Scott grew up in a small Midwestern town. A fan of storytelling from a young age, he could always be found with a book in hand. The written word fired his young mind with adventures of lands both real and imagined. He has traveled to places great and small and to this day he can still be found with his nose buried in a good book.

https://wordpress.com/view/authortlscott.wordpress.com

https://www.facebook.com/T-L-Scott-296560620394196/

https://twitter.com/TLScottAuthor

A Novel by T. L. Scott

Excerpt

Now Available on Amazon

Levels

Chapter 1

Jake leaned his head against the cool glass of the window. The air conditioning in the car was on, but it wasn't doing much. It had been in the upper nineties for the past week, and the app on his phone didn't show any change coming. Jake didn't mind the heat too much. He usually just took things in stride.

He sat forward, trying to catch some of the air blowing from the vents. It wasn't much cooler even though it was set on max chill. He arched his back, his focus fully on a bead of sweat as it rolled down his spine. He mentally tracked it all the way down to where it met his underwear and disappeared.

He sat back and rested his head against the window again, at least it felt cool. He thought about rolling it down and sticking his arm out. He imagined feeling the resistance of the wind on his hand. Mentally he cupped his hand in the current to direct some air into the car. He knew better than to ask his dad if he could roll it down. He had a thing about the noise with the windows down.

Fault Line©

Jake looked to the east as they drove across the Manchester Bridge, crossing the James River. It hadn't rained for a few weeks, and the water level was low. You could almost walk across the river, hopping from boulder to boulder out to Mayo Island.

Jake liked the sound the tires made on this part of the bridge. They sounded like they were zinging along. The sections of the bridge added a counter-point to the zinging sound. They made a rhythm as they crossed each joint: thum . . .zing… thum . . .zing… thum . . .

As much as he liked the sound as they drove, he didn't like bridges. He looked at his reflection in the window and saw a scared little boy.

It didn't happen every time, he reminded himself. He never knew when or where it would, but there was almost always something when they crossed a bridge. He forced himself to breathe deeply.

A metallic taste flooded his mouth making it fill with spit. He quickly swallowed it down. His throat clamped tight. He kept swallowing, trying to keep it under control, forcing it down his throat without puking.

A Novel by T. L. Scott

He took in a ragged breath and focused intently on something, anything, else. They had passed the mid-point of the bridge. He focused on the soothing sound of the tires and the cool feeling of the window.

He stared at the metal bridge downstream by Mayo Island. It had one train track and looked old. He had no idea just how old. He didn't even know if it was still in use. It looked cool though. The structure looked solid even if it was rusty.

"You okay back there, kiddo? Just a little bit further and we'll be over it."

Jake looked up at his dad's gaze in the rearview mirror and nodded his head. He felt it releasing its grip on him. It wasn't over, but it was passing.

It was weird. He wasn't afraid of heights. He wasn't worried about the bridge collapsing. Strangely, when the feelings hit him, he felt afraid of being alone, of being abandoned. His mind flashed to the time when he was little, and they'd been at the aquarium. He'd become separated from his dad for a few minutes. He remembered how scared he'd been, but that wasn't on a bridge. It didn't make any sense. He felt the fear rushing back as a blurry memory bubbled up. He quickly pushed it down. *That wasn't real. It didn't happen. It was nothing but your imagination. You remembered it wrong. It was probably from a nightmare, and you made it part of that time at the aquarium.*

He shook it off and sat forward again.

"Better, Jake?" asked his dad.

"Yeah," he said, relaxing his hands. The white marks on his legs began to fade where he'd been gripping them so tightly.

The buildings of downtown Richmond filled the windshield. He had always liked the look of the Federal Reserve Building. Its lines were simple and powerful. They made it look like it was soaring into the sky. The two buildings on the other side of the street, the BB&T buildings, were cool but in a different way. They were solid looking.

He felt excitement take the place of the nausea in his stomach. They were going to Wentley's department store because he needed new cleats for soccer. He knew which ones he wanted: the new model. They were so cool. They were also expensive, but he had a plan to convince his parents to let him buy them. He kept rehearsing it in his head.

He wasn't surprised his mom was still on the phone. They weren't even five minutes into the drive before it rang. It was Saturday. Couldn't she have the day off?

She looked back at him. "I'm sorry," she said putting her hand over the phone. She gave him a wink. "I'm almost done, I promise."

They'd turned into the parking garage and were cruising for an open space.

"Dad, over there, on the right," said Jake, pointing to a spot close to the entrance.

"Good eye, kiddo. This must be our lucky day."

It wasn't an ideal spot. His dad made it work though. They were between an SUV that was parked over the line and a Mini Cooper. Their car was small, but it was a good thing that the Mini Cooper was smaller yet. Jake still had to squeeze to get out of his door.

They were on the second level of the parking garage. The entrance to the store was on this level and the first one. They almost never parked on the ground floor. It was always packed with shoppers from the grocery store.

Halfway to the automatic sliding doors, his mom finally ended her call. From the sound of it, the signal had degraded to the point she couldn't hear the caller anymore. *It wasn't like she had ended it by choice,* Jake thought with uncharacteristic bitterness.

Fault Line©

"Guys, I'm sorry, but I need to finish this call. Something serious has come up," she said, already distracted.

She walked away from them, her attention fully on the phone. "I need to find a signal."

She stopped waving her phone around in search of that all elusive signal long enough to look at her family. When she saw the look on both of their faces, she took a breath and lowered the phone to her side.

"I'm sorry, but this really is important." She walked back to them and wrapped her arms through both of her guys' arms. "What do you say we grab a coffee?" She saw the looks on their faces. "I promise! I really will make it quick, okay?"

"Coffee? Yuck! I think I'll get a Red Bull instead," said Jake.

"Nice try, but no," said his dad with an eyebrow raised. "You can have a Coke instead. You know how bad those drinks are for you, Jake."

"Hey, a guy's gotta try, right?"

"Honey, you know what I want," his mom said as she brought the cell phone up to her ear. She mouthed, "I'm so sorry," waving her hand and then pointing at the phone.

Jake was already done with his Coke and it didn't look like his mom was any closer to finishing her call.

His dad took the last couple of drinks from his coffee then looked over at his wife. The only change to her soy latte was that the foam had settled. There wasn't even the tell-tale sign of her lipstick on the rim. It was evident that she hadn't even paused her conversation long enough to have a drink. It had sat there and gone cold.

Jake could tell by the frustrated look on his dad's face that he was tired of it. Like most kids his age, he knew when there was trouble at home. As much as the adults tried to keep up the appearances that everything was great, kids knew. He didn't think it was a serious problem yet, but it was getting worse.

His mom didn't notice. She was lost in her call. That was the thing with her; she was very focused. Unfortunately, the focus had been more and more on work and less and less on them.

Jake was tired of waiting. He was patient, but he was a kid.

"Dad, come on, let's just go. I bet we'll be back before she's finished."

Sadly, his dad agreed with him. He waved his hand to get her attention.

She automatically raised her index finger. "Just one more minute, honey," she mouthed before going back to her call. She hadn't even looked at him.

He'd had enough. "Let's go, son," he said standing up from the table.

She looked up at him. "I'm so sorry. Two minutes," she mouthed to him.

"We're going in," he said to her, his voice barely a whisper. He then held his pinky and thumb up in a classic call me sign.

She gave a thumbs-up and went back to her call, oblivious to his sarcasm.

"Well, kiddo, I guess it's just us for now."

They walked for a couple of minutes, merging into the flow of the other shoppers. They passed a couple of stores without saying anything to each other.

Jake felt his dad's strong hand on his shoulder.

"So, tell me again why you need those cleats?"

"Okay, first of all, the cleat pattern has been designed just for us strikers. The angle is designed for better traction for quick starts. They also made them lighter . . ." Jake went on, animatedly telling him all the reasons why he had to have them.

"So, how much do they cost?"

Jake moved to the side of the walkway, near the rail that overlooked the ground level and out of the flow of traffic. The back to school craziness had passed, and the crowds had returned to normal. At this time of the morning, foot traffic was still light.

"Dad, these are not just any shoes, alright?" Jake liked to talk with his hands when he was excited. He was using them to accentuate his points. He was so animated his dad had to fight to keep the smile off his face.

"They're really high-tech. They are designed to take the game to a whole new level. A lot of the pros are already using them." A very serious look came over him. It was time to close the deal.

"You know I need new cleats. The old ones don't fit anymore, so we have to buy a pair anyway," he reasoned, with his hands spread out from his sides for emphasis. "These shoes cost only a little more than the pair we bought last year," he quickly added.

"How much more exactly?" Derek asked.

"Thirty-three dollars."

"Jake, you do realize that's about a fifty percent increase, don't you?"

"Yeah, but, come on! I've got my own money. Between my birthday money and my allowance, I have it covered. I really need 'em."

He saw the longing on Jake's face. There was no way he could tell him no. The fact was, he'd made all the correct arguments.

He was happy and a bit sad. His son was maturing and making good choices.

He stepped forward and put his arm around Jake's shoulders. "Come on, kiddo," he said as he hugged his son to him. "Let's go shoe shopping."

"Cleats, Dad, they're called cleats, not shoes."

He squeezed his shoulder. "Okay, Jake, let's go get those cleats. Where do we need to go?"

Jake didn't bother trying to answer. He didn't know either. They walked another fifty feet before they saw a directory sign.

"Okay, it looks like we need to go to the sixth floor," his dad said. The nearest elevator was just a little bit further along the walkway.

Wentley's was basically two eight-story buildings with a two-story walkway connecting them. The walkway was enclosed from the elements with windows all around. It gave a great feeling of openness while still affording the patrons the comfort of air conditioning. Shops and small concessions, like the coffee shop they'd stopped at, were located in the center of the crossing sections.

The store they needed was on the sixth floor of the east building appropriately named East Wentley. To get to the elevator, they had to go into the clothing store on the second floor, which they were currently on.

Jake was getting frustrated. His dad was taking his time looking around the boy's section. He knew he didn't really need anything. They'd basically bought him a new wardrobe for the new school year. He had just shot up with a growth spurt over the summer, and he wasn't done with it yet. His feet had grown two sizes since July. Now that the back to school rush was over, there were some good deals on the discount displays, and he was taking his time, looking at every piece of clothing. He knew the real reason his dad was dragging his feet. It was too obvious. He was trying to give his mom time to catch up.

His dad tried to sneak a look at Jake. He was caught and judging by the look on his son's face, he was out of time. Derek stood up to his full height and let out a sigh. "Come on, kiddo. I just want to take a quick look at a pair of jeans for me before we go up."

Jake threw his hands in the air in exaggerated frustration.

"Don't worry, they're right by the elevator. I'll just be a minute."

After another ten minutes of stalling, and with a new pair of jeans in hand, Derek knew he was out of time.

"Come on, Jake. Let's go on up and get those cleats." He gave one last hopeful look at the entrance to the store before turning toward the elevator, which was to the right of the cash register where they were. The stainless-steel doors opened, discharging shoppers to continue their consumerism.

The doors closed, and the elevator departed before they reached it.

When they got to the elevator, Derek saw that the button with the up arrow was illuminated. A woman was already there waiting on the elevator to return. She was watching the floor indicator at the top of the elevator doors. An arrow pointed to the number five which was illuminated orange. The numbers were arranged in a half circle with the arrow in the center tracking the location of the elevator. He liked the look. It was a cool meeting of the old and new.

"Is there anything else we need to get while we are up there?"

Jake thought it over for a minute before answering. "I could use a new mouth guard. Oh, some soccer socks too."

He saw some color creep into Jake's cheeks as his eyes cut over to the woman. She was tall, about five ten or eleven with a strong build. She was wearing cream-colored slacks and an emerald green silk blouse. The blouse was sleeveless and showed off her well-toned arms and rich brown skin. Her thick black hair was cut to shoulder length. She stood with her hands clasped easily in front of her. Her purse, which hung off her left shoulder, was protectively held against her body by her elbow. Derek had the impression that she was a strong and steady person.

"Is there anything else?" he asked. He had a feeling Jake needed a new cup but wasn't about to say that in front of the woman.

"I'll let you know if I think of anything else."

Derek looked out of the store, back along the walkway one more time to see if he could spot her.

"She knows what we're here for. She can find us," said Jake. "We'll probably finish and find her still on the phone."

Fault Line©

Derek looked at Jake's face. It didn't look like he was upset about that. It was just something he'd come to expect from his mom.

"You know her. She's always taking care of business. It's what she's good at."

Jake smiled up at him.

Other people joined them as they waited for the elevator to arrive. A group of three teenage girls was talking about the jeans they were going to buy. The two blondes were talking with each other while the brunette, who looked to be more Jake's age, stood to the side and watched them.

A mother was trying to keep her two young children in line and hold a conversation with her father. Somehow, she was managing to pull it off.

"Mom's birthday is almost here, Dad. You should get her something nice this year. It's her sixtieth after all—Jimmy! Stay still. Mommy's talking with Grampa."

"I told you, she could use a new vacuum," her father replied.

"Dad, please be serious. She deserves to be spoiled. You need to show her how much you love her. Anna, we'll get you an ice cream for dessert, after you eat your lunch, if you behave and let Mommy and Grampa get the shopping done. Plus, Dad, she's put up with you all these years. For that alone, she deserves it," she said a bit too harshly as she exhaled a pent-up breath of frustration.

"I've been putting up with her too, mind you," he said, stubbornly staring a hole in the elevator doors.

"Stop being a grump," she said, laughing a little. "Jimmy! Stop fidgeting."

Jake kept his eyes forward and watched the drama play out in his peripheral vision. He was looking at the brunette. He didn't think she went to his school. He was sure he would remember her. He forced his eyes to look straight ahead. He didn't want to get caught checking her out.

The floor indicator showed that the car was still stopped at the fifth floor. As Jake watched, it changed to the fourth floor and stopped there.

A guy in his early twenties joined the small crowd. He stood back from the teens and off to the side. He wore glasses with round lenses, which he absentmindedly pushed back up on his nose. He looked like one of the kids from the local university. *Probably a liberal arts major*, Derek thought to himself. He was wearing jeans that ended at his ankles and no socks. He even had on a corduroy sports jacket, the kind with patches on the elbows in spite of the heat outside.

Jake always thought his dad would look good in a jacket like that. He was a writer, and he thought all writers needed to have one. Last year, he'd told his mom that he wanted to give him one for his dad's birthday. She said that it was way too cliché for a writer to actually dress like that. Still, he liked the look.

Jake took a step back. He let his eyes wander over the racks of clothing, looking for a jacket with patches on the sleeves. *It would be nice to know if they had them here*, he reasoned.

The light blinked off from the fourth floor. The arrow tracked the progress. The number three briefly flashed then finally the number two lit up. A chime sounded its arrival at their floor.

The brushed aluminum doors weren't even open all the way when a man in a brown suit bumped into his dad in his haste to depart the car.

"Excuse me," he mumbled hurrying along his way. He was a smallish man. He probably wasn't any bigger than five-two and slight of build. He was clearly in a hurry to get to wherever he was going.

Jake looked up and saw that his dad's attention was riveted on the feather sticking up from the band of the man's fedora. He watched it bob jauntily along as the man rushed off toward the exit of the store.

A few seconds passed while the rest of the passengers disembarked the elevator car. They flowed past him and the other people waiting to board. The last of the passengers cleared the car, and now, it was their turn to board.

"Come on, Dad," said Jake, nudging his side.

They followed the other passengers and boarded the car. Jake looked for the man with the hat before the doors closed, but he was gone.

They joined a group of older ladies who had stayed inside the car. The women were engaged in a conversation about, of all things, flower gardens. There were also two women in their thirties already onboard the car. They were talking about their young children.

Jake couldn't help but notice how beautiful the woman with the red hair was. Her friend was pretty, but there was something about the redhead that was very beautiful. Her skin was pale. What people called milky white. Her's wasn't pasty white, though. It was more like alabaster. It looked strong and yet still pliable. Her thick, wavy hair was anything but smooth like a model on TV. It was coarse and strong, the color of copper. It may have been the light shining down from the ceiling of the elevator car that made her hair glisten. Whatever it was, it looked beautiful. Their conversation was about their experience at a recent parent-teacher conference. From the sound of it, neither woman was pleased with the way the teachers were educating their offspring.

His dad ended up standing next to the control panel, so he asked, "Which floor, folks?" He'd already pressed the button for six. The mother said, "five, please." One of the teens said, "four."

The other passengers must have been satisfied with the selections as they didn't add any further destinations to the itinerary.

The doors began to slide closed.

"Hold the door, please," called out a male voice.

Derek pushed the button to reopen the doors. They continued to slide closed. He confirmed that he had pushed the right button. Sure enough, it had been the one with the arrows pointed toward each other. Satisfied that his selection was now correct, he stabbed it in rapid succession. The antiquated doors finally got the message and reversed their progress.

"Thank you," said the man as he stepped aboard. He was easily in his sixties, maybe even in his seventies. It was hard to tell. He was about five-six and of average build. He wore a goatee on his dark-skinned face and was dressed in khaki pants and a polo shirt with a blue blazer. The smile he flashed his dad revealed a set of very white teeth.

"No problem, sir," he replied.

The doors stayed in the open position for another twenty seconds or so before cycling to close again. Jake observed the other passengers. The teen girls were still actively engaged in their conversation. The subject had changed from jeans to shoes. Undoubtedly, this was a dramatic shift in their world but only a minuscule shift for everyone else. The mother was making suggestions to her father on what would make a good present for his loving wife. The rest of the passengers were doing what passengers who don't know each other do when in such a confined space. They were looking anywhere but at each other. Most of the people, Jake could see, were looking at the floor indicator above the doors.

Finishing the path of their cycle, the doors closed with a dull *thunk*. Five seconds turned to ten, but there was no discernable movement. He looked down to make sure the light for the fourth floor had been pushed. The button was still lit up.

Fault Line©

Another few seconds went by, but still, there was no change. He saw a few of the other passengers looking at the floor buttons, as he had done. Finally, the doors began to slide open again. They were still at two.

The mother stepped out of the elevator, still involved in her conversation with her dad.

"Ma'am," said Jake to get her attention. "I think we're still on the second floor."

They looked around and saw that it all looked the same.

"I guess I wasn't paying attention," she said laughing as she re-boarded the car.

His dad pressed the button to close the doors again. Everyone watched as they proceeded on their track. The same reassuring *thunk* sounded when they met. The same awkward amount of time passed before the doors opened again. This time they had all been watching the floor indicator and noted that no change had occurred. Things outside of the car looked the same.

"Well, that's odd," said the young college student.

His dad pushed the button for the doors to close again.

Odd is the right word. Something was troubling Jake. He couldn't quite place it, but something was off. He reached over and held his dad's hand. The doors were almost closed when his gaze fell on the young woman that had operated the register when his dad paid for his jeans. She was pregnant. Obviously pregnant too, at least seven or eight months along. He could have sworn she hadn't been when she'd sold him the jeans.

The same sound of the doors meeting and the same pause after they closed. He felt the added gravity pushing down on him. The elevator was finally moving. They looked at each other, exchanging relieved smiles. The kind that said: I wasn't worried; even though we know I kind of was.

The floor indicator bar went out for two, and the three lit up. The car slowed, easing to a stop. Derek saw some of his fellow passengers looked at the control panel. The button for the third floor wasn't lit. He hadn't pushed it.

Fault Line©

Chapter 2

Jake gripped his dad's hand tightly.

Derek squeezed his hand back and leaned down toward him. It wasn't like he had far to go. He marveled at how quickly his little boy was growing up. *Fourteen already! Where have the years gone?*

"It's just a little delay, kiddo. We'll get you those shoes in no time."

Jake looked up at him. Derek was surprised to see fear on his young face. He leaned in a little closer.

"What's wrong, son?"

"I don't know. Something feels bad."

Derek's mind cast back to another time. Jake was six and had wanted to see the dolphins. He was interested in animals, all kinds of animals. They'd already seen most of the exhibits. He'd really enjoyed watching the alligators being fed. They were really slow until the food was thrown, in then they went crazy, thrashing around and rolling over each other to get at the food. The show they'd really gone to see was going to start in about 15 minutes. They were below the seating level looking into the big tank. The dolphins were already performing. They were swimming by the glass performing for their audience.

School was out because of a teacher administrative day. A day for the teachers to catch up on their admin meant a day for the kids to have some fun.

They'd been watching the dolphins for a little over five minutes. He'd felt good standing there holding his little boy's hand. As much as he'd wanted the moment to last, he knew it couldn't. He'd checked his watch. He didn't want to rush to find a seat for the show. He figured they had another five minutes. He was surprised Jake hadn't gotten bored yet. Six-year-old boys didn't usually have much of an attention span. Something caught Jake's attention. He'd turned from the tank, trying to look everywhere at once it seemed. He was squeezing Derek's hand tightly.

"What is it, son?"

"I don't know dad. Something feels bad."

"Do you need to go to the bathroom?"

"No, not that. Something feels weird," Jake said, scrunching up his shoulders.

A woman was standing to their left. She was struggling to keep her little boy and girl from fighting. Derek could hear in her voice how much of a challenge it was for her to keep her patience. Derek had to give her credit. He sometimes felt stressed looking after Jake. He couldn't imagine trying to take care of three kids at the same time. She was handling the situation well, managing two toddler's temperaments and handling the needs of an infant in a stroller.

The mother's attention was fully focused on the little girl. She was throwing a fit, claiming the boy had pinched her arm. That was when the baby in the stroller tossed her toy onto the ground.

Wanting to help his fellow parent, Derek had reached down to retrieve it for the tired mother.

"Thank you," she'd said.

He could tell by her expression that she'd appreciated the small act of kindness. More than that he could see she appreciated that someone else understood how difficult her day was.

"It's really no problem, ma'am," he had assured her.

Jake was gone. He'd just let go of his hand for a second.

Derek had frantically looked around. He couldn't have gone far. The crowd was light. There were less than ten people standing around. He hadn't seen his son anywhere. Jake was wearing a red jacket. He should have been able to spot him right away. Derek had hurried around the exhibit, not quite running. *Maybe he wandered around the side to get a better look*, he thought. *Oh, God help me. Where are you, Jake?*

Derek hadn't see him anywhere. His fear had threatened to overwhelm him. He was breathing fast. Derek doubled back to the side of the enclosure they'd been standing at.

Jake wasn't there. He'd forced himself to scan the area slowly, trying to make sure he wouldn't miss anything. It hadn't helped that the lights were dimmed so you could see inside the tank better.

He'd checked the area as thoroughly as he could.

No Jake.

The sharp teeth of panic had gnawed on his senses. He was breathing fast. His eyes darted everywhere, trying to catch a glimpse of his son. *This can't be happening. He can't be gone. Not my Jake.*

He'd felt sick. Sweat beaded on his upper lip. His throat had clamped down to a tiny opening. He couldn't take a deep breath. He'd felt sure he was going to vomit. He had to find Jake.

"Have you seen a little boy? He has blond hair. He's wearing a red jacket with a hood and jeans." He'd asked anyone he could.

He'd seen an employee and ran over to her.

"Excuse me, ma'am. I can't find my son. He was standing right there with me," he'd said, pointing to where Jake had been. "He was there, holding my hand and then he was just gone."

"I'm sure he's fine, sir," she'd replied confidently. "I'm going to call this in." She'd unclipped the radio from her belt. "Maybe he's already been found by another employee and is sitting safe and sound in one of our offices," she'd said trying to reassure him.

"What does he look like, sir?"

Derek had given her Jake's description.

"Central, this is Shirley, we have a report of a lost boy. His father reports that the child is six years old, blond hair, wearing jeans and a red hooded jacket. The boy's name is Jacob."

"He goes by Jake."

"Central, the boy goes by Jake."

"Roger that, Shirley. We'll let you know when we find him."

"Okay, sir, we have his description, and every employee is going to be looking out for him. We're actually pretty good at this," she'd said reassuringly. "It happens more often than you think. Kids are curious. Sometimes they wander off, chasing something that caught their interest. I'm sure we'll find him in no time."

Derek had nodded his head. He'd felt numb all over. He couldn't think clearly. All he could think about was that he had to find Jake. Nothing else mattered.

"Sir, would you like to come with me? You can wait in the administrative offices," she'd said with genuine concern. "That way, as soon as any word about your son comes in, we can let you know." She'd noted the lost look on his face. She'd seen that look enough times in the two years she'd been working there. In almost every case, they'd been successful in reuniting the family.

"No, thank you, I need to stay here. He could come back looking for me."

The woman looked at him kindly. She reached up and squeezed his shoulder. "We'll find him, sir," she'd said reassuringly.

Derek had thanked her and walked back over to stand in front of the tank. The dolphins had stopped swimming around. They were staying still. It looked like they were watching Derek. The only movement they'd made was to move their heads from side to side.

Fault Line©

One of the larger dolphins turned to the side and moved closer to the glass. He was right in front of Derek. They looked at each other eye to eye.

Derek had been transfixed. He'd felt like he was being pulled into that intelligent gaze. He'd had no sense of time passing. Even his anxiety over Jake had subsided for a moment.

Derek marveled at how much intelligence he felt looking back at him. He'd felt like he was being analyzed. The dolphin looked like he'd been in deep thought as if he was puzzling over something. Maybe he was. Maybe he'd been thinking about why the people were there.

He'd stood there, lost, for a while, looking back at the big male staring at him. He'd felt completely lost. He didn't know what else he could do. He couldn't think straight. He'd replayed in his mind what had happened over and over again. He'd tried in vain to see what had happened. How he could have been separated from Jake.

He'd picked up a subtle change in the animal's expression a split second before it broke contact and looked down.

Something had slammed into the side of his leg. The force of the impact had almost knocked him off his feet.

He'd stumbled a couple of shuffling steps to the left pinwheeling his arms to catch his balance. He'd been stunned to see the top of Jake's head. His little face had been pressed so hard against Derek's thigh, arms wrapped around his legs, holding tight.

Derek had kneeled down and wrapped Jake in his arms.

"Where were you?" Jake had choked out the question between his panicked sobs.

"Where did you go, Daddy? I was so scared. Why'd you leave me?"

Derek had gently pushed his son back, so he could see his face. Tears streamed down his chubby cheeks. His whole body was wracked with the force of his sobbing.

"I didn't leave you. I've been right here. Where did you go?" Derek had asked, confused.

"I didn't go anywhere, Daddy. I stayed right here. I felt you let go of my hand and then you were gone. Where did you go? I was so scared. I didn't move. Just like you said. I didn't move. I stayed right here and waited for you to find me. Why did you leave me? Everybody was gone, Daddy. Where did everybody go?"

Derek had been confused. He didn't understand what had just happened. The only thing he knew, the only thing that mattered, was that Jake was okay. He'd picked him up and hugged him tight to his chest.

"It's okay now, son. Everything's going to be okay."

Derek had held onto him tightly. He'd looked back at the tank. The dolphins had gone away.

Derek had never found out what had happened that day. He'd written it off to Jake being scared and disoriented. He'd been grateful that nothing worse had happened.

Derek's senses were on high alert. The memory of that day kicked his protective instincts into high gear.

The elevator was not quick. It took a few seconds for the door to open onto the third floor. A sign hanging from the ceiling directed patrons to the sections they were interested in. An arrow for bedding and linens pointed straight ahead. Bathroom and other household items were to the left. Draperies and blinds to the right. Derek saw the bedding displays. The section was in the center of the store. The aisle went around the central circle. Inside, draperies were hung from false walls hanging to the side of simulated windows. Pictures were mounted, tastefully accentuating the display. It was all designed to give the impression of what your bedroom could look like if you bought the ensemble, the whole ensemble.

To the left, towels and bath rugs were on display. Farther along, sheets and bedding ensembles were prominently positioned on the shelves lining the aisles. To the right, pots and pans adorned the stove tops of simulated kitchens.

All along the back of the floor, furthest from the elevator, living room furniture was showcased. Couches, lamps, and end tables were set up to simulate the living room you wanted to come home to. Warm light bathed the staged room. He saw one display that had a picture of a football game on the TV set prominently in the center of the room.

A young man was standing in front of the open elevator doors, waiting to board. He was dressed in a pair of gray slacks, a white shirt, and a simple gray tie. He had on plain black shoes. His hair was neatly combed to the side. He looked to be about Jake's age. It was kind of odd, Derek thought, for a boy of his age to be dressed that way, especially on a Saturday morning. He looked so proper. It was in stark contrast to the ongoing trend of sagging.

The passengers already on the elevator stepped back to make room for the boy. Derek noticed the boy looking at the other passengers, especially the teenage girls. When his eyes found Jake, Derek saw the questioning look on his face.

Derek's attention went back to the scene outside of the now closing elevator doors. He noticed that the shoppers were dressed like the new passenger. The ladies were wearing knee-length skirts, and the men were in dress slacks or suits. Even the children were dressed that way.

The doors eased closed and made the now familiar *thunk* sound.

He turned his attention to the new passenger, looking at him out of the corner of his eye. The boy stood as close to the door as he could, as far away from the other passengers as possible. His hands held rigidly down by his sides, not in his pockets. His whole demeanor was stiff. His discomfort was palpable.

Derek's imagination was hard at work trying to figure out what was going on. What could be the reason this boy was dressed like he was? Why would the other shoppers on the third floor be dressed the same way? Sure, some of them could be expected to be dressed up for different reasons. The adults anyway. They could be working on a Saturday or maybe they just normally dressed that way. Some of the kids could be explained in the same way. Maybe their parents just dressed them that way. It wasn't so easy to understand why all of them would be dressed like that though. *Maybe they just came from a wedding?* He thought. *No*, he rejected that scenario. *It was too early in the day for that. Maybe they were all going to a dance recital.* The performing arts theater wasn't far away. *Maybe they were putting on a noon performance.* That was possible, except he knew that at least some of the people would have been wearing jeans.

As hard as he tried, he couldn't fit what he saw with any solid explanation. It wasn't that it was strange for people to dress that way. It was just strange that so many of them would be dressed the same way. It was almost like pictures he had seen from the fifties and sixties.

The car rose on its cable. "Here we go, Jake," he said, giving his hand a gentle squeeze. The floor indicator changed to four. Derek turned his shoulder, preparing to step out once the doors opened. He moved behind Jake and put his hands on his shoulders, ready to follow him.

The elevator didn't slow. The indicator light for four went out. Derek looked down at the control panel and saw that the light there was still glowing its dirty yellow light. He looked over at the other passengers. Some of them were obviously dismayed as well.

Jake looked up at him. He was scared.

Derek couldn't tell if he was feeling spooked by his son's fear or if he was feeling something ominous as well. In the end, it didn't matter. He needed to keep Jake safe. If that meant calming his fears, okay. If it meant protecting him from something else, then that was what he would do.

The ascent of the car changed, slowing as it approached the fifth floor. The indicator above the door illuminated the number five. Derek unconsciously tensed his muscles in anticipation of what might happen.

The car came to a halt, and the doors slowly slid open onto the women's department. Prominently on display in the center of the floor were the jewelry and perfume display cases. The area was bathed in clean white light. Customers were scattered around the glass cases browsing the items on display.

The area to the left was the section for makeup products. Customers were sitting on stools while employees in white smocks danced around them with brushes in hand working their art on the canvas of their faces.

Derek saw a few men standing nearby trying to look interested in the process. Some of them had given up the effort and were focused on their phones instead.

Everything looked normal here. The woman with her father and children got off the elevator and made their way toward the center counter. *It looks like Grandma's going to get either jewelry or some perfume.*

Nobody was waiting to board the elevator, so Derek took the opportunity to poke his head out and look around. Nothing looked out of the ordinary. Everyone was dressed and acting as he expected. It looked, for lack of a better word, normal.

He stepped back into the elevator and looked around at the other passengers. "Nobody else?" he asked. No one wanted to get off, so he pushed the button to close the doors. He reached down and took Jake's hand in his again. He figured the car would go up to the sixth floor next. He wanted to get the cleats for Jake and get back to Julie.

The button for five hadn't been pressed and was still not lit up. It made sense the car would continue in the same direction it had been going. In this case, to continue going up before going back down again.

Fault Line©

The doors went through their cycle again, including the solid *thunk* when they met. He waited for the feeling of the car rising up the cable. The seconds ticked by. Ten seconds went by with nothing happening. Ten seconds normally is not a long time, but when you are in an enclosed space, looking at a set of closed doors, and waiting for something to happen, time stretches out.

Finally, something happened. The doors began to open again. His eyes, as well as most of the other passengers, went up to the floor indicator, even though he knew they hadn't moved. Sure enough, it still said they were on five.

The passengers looked around at each other. Most were smiling a little. The elevators were old. Even though the buildings had been completely refurbished during the last upgrade, they had kept the original elevator cars. They wanted to keep as much of the historic buildings as possible. Everyone understood that sometimes glitches happened. It was the price to pay for patching the past and present together.

Again, there wasn't anyone waiting on the car. That would have explained it. If someone had pushed the call button, then it might have opened for them. But there wasn't anyone there.

Derek took a step out of the elevator and looked to each side. He didn't see anything to explain why the elevator hadn't moved. He shrugged his shoulders and stepped back into the car then pushed the button to close the doors again. They went through their cycle, and again, they didn't go anywhere. The doors opened to the same scene.

The woman in the emerald green blouse stepped forward. "I don't know about you guys, but this isn't normal."

"What are you going to do?" asked the man with the goatee.

"I'm going to ask one of the employees if there's something wrong with the elevator." She had a confident, purposeful stride. Her heels clicked on the tile flooring as she walked to the jewelry counter at the center of the floor.

Derek decided to follow her. "Come on, Jake," he said, gently pushing him forward by the shoulders.

Jake was looking around at the displays lining the aisle they were walking down. Box sets of men's and women's perfumes and bath products lined both sides of the aisle. Down the center, prominently displayed, were fragrances endorsed by celebrities. Banners with their perfect faces hung suspended over the products.

Derek recognized a few of them. He wasn't one to keep up with the tabloids, so he wasn't surprised that there were some he didn't know.

Muted footfalls caught Jake's attention, so he turned and glanced over his shoulder. The fellow with the goatee was following close behind them.

"Might as well try and find out what's going on," the man said with a small shrug of his shoulders.

Derek recognized the mother with her father and children. She was talking with one of the sales representatives over on the far side of the jewelry cases. From the look of things, she wasn't having much success convincing her dad.

The woman in the emerald green blouse had arrived at the counter and was waiting to speak with a store employee. They were all busy with customers.

Derek took advantage of the situation and engaged her in conversation.

"Ma'am, excuse me," he said to get her attention.

"Oh, hi," she responded.

"What do you think is going on?"

"It's probably just what it seems to be, probably nothing more than old equipment that's been in service too long," she said with a little smile.

That sounded reasonable. Except why was she going to talk with an employee if it was that simple?

She answered as if she had been reading his mind.

"I just think there's a small chance that this could be the start of a problem with the elevator. If they know about it, maybe they can get it fixed before someone gets stuck between floors. Trust me, that's no fun."

"How long were you stuck there?" Jake asked her.

"It wasn't very long, sweetie," she said looking down at him with a smile. "They were able to get the car moving again in no time."

She probably has a son too, thought Derek. She had effortlessly eased any possible anxiety Jake may have had about getting back on an elevator.

The look she gave Derek confirmed his suspicion. She'd been stuck in that elevator much longer than she had liked. She was trying to do something to avoid it from happening to someone else.

Fault Line©

Seeing one of the clerks finishing up, Derek raised his hand and waved to get her attention.

"How can I help you?" she asked stepping closer to them.

Derek inclined his head toward the businesswoman. She took his cue.

"We were just on the elevator, and it's acting a bit strange."

The woman sighed. "I'm sorry about that. Those old cars are always having issues. What happened?" she asked.

They told her what had happened, and the clerk nodded her head in understanding. "I'm sorry to say, but that is pretty normal. They're safe to use. Fortunately, they don't break down on us too often. When they have broken down, they usually come right back up." She flashed them a smile that was meant to be reassuring. Unfortunately, it conveyed too much of how tired she was of talking about the elevator. She stood a little straighter and tried to inject more sincerity into her voice. "I appreciate you letting us know. I'll call maintenance, so they can look into it. Is there anything else I can help you with?" she asked with a small smile.

"No, thank you."

"Okay, you all have a nice time and thank you for shopping at Wentley's."

They turned and walked a couple of steps away from the counter. The businesswoman slowed to a stop.

Curious, Derek did as well. "What is it?"

"I'm not sure," she said. "It's probably nothing."

Derek just looked at her and waited. The gentleman with the goatee was also standing off to the side, waiting for her response.

"Did you see the perfume displays?"

Each of the guys nodded their head and turned to look over at the displays.

"Maybe you didn't notice, but one was a contestant on one of those singing reality shows. The thing is, she shouldn't be on that display. She didn't win. In fact, she didn't even place in the top ten. She wasn't very good, and her attitude was terrible. There's no way she got that endorsement. It's just wrong."

Once she explained who the woman on the display was, Derek recognized her. He'd watched a few episodes and agreed with the woman's assessment. He also thought that she looked pretty plain. She wasn't ugly, but she wasn't pretty enough to overcome the points the woman made against her being on that display. He chose to keep his thoughts to himself.

The guy with the goatee was nodding his head. "That does sound odd. Did you notice the clothes our young friend is wearing? The one that's about your age, young man," he said looking at Jake.

"Yeah," answered Derek. The woman was also nodding her head.

"Did you also notice how the other shoppers were dressed on the floor when he got on with us?"

"I thought that was weird too," answered the woman. "Why would they all be dressed that way?"

"Did you notice the small man in the brown suit and fedora?" Derek asked.

"What's odd about that?" asked the goateed gentleman. "I wear a fedora myself from time to time."

"Yeah, I understand," he answered. "I don't know; it just felt a little strange is all. I don't know how to say it any better than that."

The woman was looking over Derek's shoulder, back toward the elevator. He turned and looked too. The doors were still open. Most of the other passengers were still inside the car. A few people had gathered just inside the store.

"Okay, that's strange. Maybe it's broken down now," she said. "I'm going to go find the stairs." She turned on her sensibly heeled tan shoes and walked off.

"You know, Jake, that sounds like a good idea. Let's look around for a little bit while we're here."

"Do you mind if I follow along?" asked the man.

"Sure, I'm Derek, and this is my son Jake," he said, reaching out his hand to shake the other man's.

"Pleased to meet you. My name is Khalid."

"Okay, so, she said that the display for that perfume was wrong. What if we go around and see if anything else looks, well, off?"

Khalid and Jake both nodded their heads that they agreed. Since the woman had gone to the left, they decided to go to the right to see what they could find, if anything.

"Stay close to me, Jake."

They roamed around the store, looking at the different merchandise. Derek admitted to himself that he was at a disadvantage. He had never been the guy that was interested in colognes and perfumes.

Fault Line©

At the back of the store, a section was set aside for the display of crystal bowls and decanters, Faberge eggs, and other gift type items. Derek stopped to examine a display for some interestingly designed cat figurines.

Julie had started a collection a few years back. Her favorite artist was Stromzin. Derek was happy to see that several of the items on display were ones she didn't have yet. He was kind of surprised because he'd been buying them for her and thought he recognized the whole catalog. Maybe these were a new collection. He turned the figurine over and looked at the label on the bottom. He almost dropped it in his surprise. *This must be a mistake. There's no way that this costs eight hundred and forty-five dollars.* The last time he bought one, it was only forty-seven, fifty. Curious, he looked at the other pieces and saw that they were similarly priced. *Maybe this is a limited edition or something. There's no way I'm spending that much.* He carefully put it back down.

Jake was looking at a display of miniature antique car replicas. "See anything you like?" Derek asked him.

"Look at this, Dad." Jake handed him a white car with teal trim.

A Novel by T. L. Scott

Derek knew enough to know that it was an early 1950s model. He was good at recognizing the cars from this timeframe. He didn't recognize this one, though. He looked closer at the plaque: 1953 Atwood Airstream. He was puzzled. He'd never heard of a company called Atwood. He looked around and saw Khalid a few feet away. He brought the car over to him.

"Hey, have you ever heard of an Atwood Airstream?" he asked him, handing the car over.

Khalid shook his head as he looked over the model. "It looks like a Buick, but not quite. The fins are too flared at the back and look here," he said pointing at the grill. "I have never seen a car with a symbol like this, A. Are these supposed to be models of real cars?" he asked.

Jake led him back to the display. Khalid took a few minutes looking over the other models without saying anything. After a couple of minutes had gone by, he stood back up to his full height.

"There are a few that I don't recognize at all. Some, I recognize, but there are a few things about them that are a little bit different, though. There's something off about them. Look here," he said, pointing to a 1964 Cadillac Convertible. "The hood is flat. It's supposed to be curved with a scoop on it. There're more models like the Atwood. Models I don't recognize as ever being produced. There's a chance these are foreign cars. Not much of one, though. I know a lot about the cars of this time. I have a Bellaire that I restored and show at car shows. It's a hobby of mine. Now that I'm retired I have learned a lot about these cars."

"So, what do you think it means?" Derek asked.

"I don't know," Khalid answered, shaking his head slowly.

Derek liked this man. He felt that he could trust him. He sounded like a serious man that wasn't prone to fantasy.

"I think we should keep looking around. That woman went to go find the stairs. Maybe we should do the same," Khalid suggested as he cast his eyes to the other side of the store.

That sounded like a good idea to Derek. As good an idea as any at this point anyway. Things definitely felt strange, but thankfully, he didn't think that they were in any immediate danger.

He looked back to the elevator. It was still there, doors standing wide open. The young scholar and the boy in the tie were standing inside the car talking with each other. The two older women were just outside, to the right of the car. The other passengers must have wandered off.

Derek looked around and spotted the three teenage girls over by the Sofe' display. The mother and father were looking over another selection of perfumes. Her children were looking into the display cases as only children do. They had their little noses pressed right on the glass. Derek couldn't suppress his smile as they walked past the kids. Jake used to do the same thing when he was little.

On their way across the store, they saw the woman in the emerald green blouse looking out the window. Curious, Derek decided to go and see what she was looking at.

When they were still a good ten feet away, she turned and watched them approach.

"Hello again," said Derek in greeting.

"Have you seen anything interesting?" asked Khalid.

"Well, for starters, the stairwell isn't accessible. They are doing work on the fire main, or so the sign says. There's scaffolding blocking the door from opening so we can't use the stairs."

"That's very strange," said Khalid. "That's a major fire code violation."

Fault Line©

She nodded her head. "My thought exactly. You can also forget the windows. They don't open," she said pointing to the place the glass met the frame.

Derek tapped his finger on the glass. The tone sounded strange.

"You guessed it," she said. "Some type of plastic."

He leaned in closer and looked at the pane. "It's one of those energy efficient windows, there are actually three panes inside," he said.

"They must have put them in during the renovation," said Khalid.

He looked at the woman and reached out his hand to her. "I'm Khalid."

She shook his hand. "Nancy," she replied.

"I'm Derek, and this is my son, Jake," he said.

Khalid filled her in on the things they had observed.

While he was talking, Derek let his eyes wander to the scene outside the window.

Traffic was flowing by, both on the road and on the sidewalks. He stepped closer to the window and looked down to get a good look at the pedestrians on this side of the road. He didn't know what he had expected. Maybe a blurred line that separated the building from the rest of the world. Something that looked strange that would explain why they were different in here. Maybe even a film crew. Things were weird enough, maybe they'd stepped into a reality show and would all sign waivers and release forms.

There was no blurred line, no TV crew, no visible explanation to put this all on.

He let his eyes wander over the scene below. From this height, it all looked like something out of a movie. Everything was orderly and neat. There wasn't any trash in the gutters. There weren't any bums looking for handouts. He didn't see any graffiti marking the walls. He was looking to his right when he saw two men walking side by side. What had drawn his attention to them was that they were wearing identical black uniforms with tall black boots. Each of the men had a black beret, tilted to the side, on his head. The crowds of people flowed around them as water in a stream flows past a boulder. No one came closer to them than a few feet. He didn't know what to make of the two men.

He noticed that Nancy had moved next to him. "I see our friends are back again."

"Who are they?" asked Derek.

"I'm not sure, but they act like beat cops," she replied.

Fault Line©

"I've never seen any police uniforms like that," said Derek.

"Me either," agreed Khalid. He had his face pressed so close to the window that his breath was fogging it up when he exhaled.

They watched the pair of men as they continued on their way. Across the street, a bus pulled away from its stop. On the side of the enclosure, a sign caught Derek's attention: Curfew Strictly Enforced. Under those words, an official-looking badge, like a police badge, was displayed.

Derek had seen enough. Whatever was going on was not confined to this building. It didn't matter if they found a way down or not. Things were not the same.

"What in the hell is going on?" he muttered.

Jake looked up at him. It wasn't like his dad to use that kind of language.

"I don't know about you, but I'm going to go back to the elevator and try to get out of here," said Nancy.

"I don't think that's going to make any difference," said Khalid. "Things aren't normal outside. I don't know about you guys, but when I came into the store we didn't have a curfew, and

I know we didn't have men in all black uniforms and jackboots patrolling the streets."

"Okay then, what do you propose we do?" she asked.

"While I stick to what I said, I don't think it's going to make any difference, but I don't have any better ideas. Nancy, I think your idea is the best one we have," said Khalid.

Derek agreed. He didn't see any better options. Staying here was only continuing with this strange reality they were in.

"Hey, Dad …"

"It'll be okay, son. We'll figure this out."

"The elevator's gone."

They all looked across the store at the shiny metal doors. No one was standing near them.

Derek looked at Nancy and Khalid. He didn't see fear on their faces, but it wasn't far away, he thought.

"I don't know about you, but I think it's time for us to go," she said as she set off walking.

The rest of the group fell in stride behind her. Derek looked around for any of the people they had arrived with. He didn't know how he would go about explaining things to them, but he knew he didn't want to leave anyone behind.

Fault Line©

The family that had been shopping for a gift was nowhere to be seen. Derek looked around as they made their way past the jewelry counter and proceeded to close the distance to the elevator. There were parts of the store they couldn't see because of the way the displays were set up. He didn't feel like wasting time looking around. As much as he didn't want to leave any of the other passengers behind, his priority was Jake and he felt a sense of urgency. He felt the need to get away from there as soon as possible.

They were still a good thirty or so feet away from the elevator when Derek saw that the floor indicator wasn't lit. *Maybe it's in between floors.* He kept his eyes on the display while they closed the distance. The small group slowed as they arrived at the elevator. The lights above the doors remained dark. No one said anything. They just stood there looking up. After what felt like a long time the indicator for five lit up, and the doors began to open. Their fellow passengers were still inside the car. Everyone except the mother with her children and father.

The little old lady in the dress with the yellow flowers spoke up. "This elevator is not working well at all," she said to her friend. "We should take the stairs."

"You know we can't do that, dear. My hip simply will not allow me to."

"Well, this elevator isn't getting us anywhere. Look, we're right back on five again. If we don't hurry and get our shopping done, we'll be late for tea."

"I'm sure we still have plenty of time," her friend reassured her.

They made room for Derek's group to re-board the car. The college kid was now standing next to the control panel.

Jake looked at it and saw that the lights for seven and eight were lit in addition to six. Two and one had also been pushed. *Okay, which will it be? Up or down?* The doors slowly closed. *And what will we find when we get there?*

Made in the USA
Middletown, DE
04 February 2019